The Nun in a Chemise

Curious Conversations

Venus in the Cloister

or

The Nun in a Chemise

Curious Conversations

Abbé du Prat

Translated by Andrew Brown

Published by Hesperus Press Limited
28 Mortimer Street, London W1W 7RD
www.hesperuspress.com

First published in French, 1683
First published by Hesperus Press Limited, 2012

Introduction and English language translation © Andrew Brown, 2012

Designed and typeset by Fraser Muggeridge studio
Printed in Jordan by Jordan National Press

ISBN: 978-1-84391-192-0

CONTENTS

It seems rather superfluous to write an introduction to a piece of pornography. Why not just get down to it?

Many years ago I told the teacher in a French school where I was the English language assistant how I planned to start work with a new class. I would begin, I informed her, by introducing myself – but I mistakenly used the word '*m'introduire*', which has a rather different sense in French: it sounded as if I were planning to 'insert myself' into the pupils. She kindly pointed out that this would not get things off to the best start ('That's exactly the kind of thing that will make them giggle [*rigoler*]').

Why, here, should I '*introduire*' (or even '*présenter*', the correct word) a text that speaks for itself? The reader is welcome to head straight for the cloisters; the tale needs no introduction. It's the *real thing* (there is, after all, nothing more real than pornography).

Still, by way of foreplay, here – in no particular order – are a few themes that the reader might like to ponder while turning the pages with one hand, and a few thoughts that occurred to me as I typed out my translation with the other.

Authors

Nobody knows for sure who wrote *Venus in the Cloister*, or when.

One candidate is Jean Barrin (1640–1718). He translated Ovid into French, and so may well have had a liking for licentious writing in general.

Another possible author of the work was François de Chavigny de La Bretonnière (1652–98). Born in Paris, he was forced into the Congrégation de Saint-Maur and took his vows as a Benedictine in 1671, at the age of nineteen. He was later at the Abbey of Saint-Germain-des-Prés, from which he fled having stolen 600 *pistoles*, and took up residence in Holland; we hear of him in 1682 in Amsterdam, the capital of European freethinking – though even here he was soon in trouble for publishing subversive pamphlets and short stories. Apparently, he could earn twenty-two livres per week for writing satirical sketches in the French-language newspapers of Amsterdam. But he went bankrupt and was constantly having run-ins with the law, though he just as constantly refused to attend the summonses which were issued. In 1684, he wrote a virulent satire against the Archbishop of Reims, *Le cochon mitré* (*The Pig in a Mitre*). He was arrested for this, denied having written it, and was released. In 1685, according to one account, there was a plan to accuse him of magical practices. His journalism attacked the expansionist and absolutist policies of Louis XIV, and showed sympathy for France's beleaguered Protestants. He may well have been a friend of Gabriel de Ceinglen (the colleague and translator of Spinoza, whose meditations on man as part of Nature cast their bright shadow across the most advanced speculations of the next three centuries, and are echoed in certain passages of *Venus in the Cloister*). Eventually, Chavigny was lured into a trap and taken back to France, and interned temporarily in the Bastille before being handed back to his Benedictine superiors. These were obviously not inclined to treat their prodigal son with any indulgence: instead, they sent him to Mont Saint-Michel, which was not only an abbey but a prison as well. He was locked away in a narrow wooden cage, where he languished for thirteen years. (Others say he was given relative liberty.) By the time he was released, in 1698, he was mad. He died shortly afterwards.

None of the preceding facts (especially the dates) are entirely secure.

Several anonymous works are attributed to him, and he (or someone else) actually put his name to various others, whose general tenor can be seen from their titles: *Sophia, or the Venetian Widow*; *The Hermaphrodite in Love*; *Octavia, or the Unfaithful Wife*. He may also have written *The Fake Abbess, or the Duped Suitor*; *The Artificial Mistress, or His Own Rival*; and *Conversations at the Grille, or the Monk in the Parlour*. As these titles suggest, Chavigny's interests covered both the erotic and the religious life, especially when they intersected. So – as many scholars have concluded – he is more than likely to have produced *Venus in the Cloister*.

But the best solution is simply to say that the work was written by the Abbé du Prat. ('Nice name he has,' an English-speaking reader might remark.) Or, even more simply, that this tale of nuns was written by Anon.

Dialogue
Venus in the Cloister is a dialogue, and, like Plato's dialogues, it raises profound philosophical questions. Also like Plato's dialogues, it sometimes goes off at a tangent, includes short stories, indulges in banter, or flirtation, or private jokes, or alludes to matters that made better sense to a contemporary reader than to us. Admittedly, there is more kissing in *Venus in the Cloister* than in Plato (but just as much homoeroticism in Plato as in *Venus in the Cloister*). Readers of *Venus in the Cloister* will be able to follow trains of argument that touch on cultural and ethical relativism, patriarchy, the relationship between the true church and its corrupt institutions, the nature of the mystical, the allure of books, and the relation between the so-called private and public realms. They can ponder the way the apparent tranquillity of the cloisters (its poverty, chastity and obedience), seemingly so far removed

from the hubbub of the world, actually mirrors, in magnified and inverted form, the world's power and lust. Quicker than a nun can change her chemise, they will glimpse the mystery of transcendence: how the bodily at its most intensely profane seems indistinguishable from the sacred – unless, of course, this is an illusion created by the Devil.

(Aretino's erotic works also mix the amorous and the philosophical in dialogue form: both his *The Secret Life of Nuns* and *Venus in the Cloister* are works of pornosophy.)

Editions

The first (1683) edition of *Venus in the Cloister* had just three dialogues; the second (1702) added two more; the third, in 1719, had a sixth dialogue with two new interlocutors. In fact, this is a gross simplification: the publishing history of the book is extremely vexed, as so often with *libertin* writings. The date and place of publication of subversive or licentious works was, especially in the seventeenth and eighteenth centuries, often falsely given so as to put censors and potential prosecutors off the trail. In particular, publication was frequently post-dated. There are editions of *Vénus dans le Cloître* dated 1683 and 1685, and others 1719, but some references in the text suggest that it was probably published in the early eighteenth century. The story of the man who disguises himself as a nun to gain access to the convent, found in the fifth dialogue, may be inspired by a story by La Fontaine (1674), though it is surely a much older theme than that. The first three dialogues seem to hang together, with the later two (or three) being additions, perhaps apocryphal. Dialogues always involve more than two people (Freud said the same about sex).

Enlightenment

Venus in the Cloister refers on several occasions to 'light', and once to 'enlightenment' (*les lumières*). It was written as one of the myriad underground texts – anti-clerical, anti-monarchist, often epicurean, materialistic or sceptical in philosophy, frequently pornographic – that circulated in Europe in increasing numbers from the end of the seventeenth century. They were part of the intellectual ferment that produced, among other things, the French Revolution. *Venus in the Cloister* is a short treatise on the policing of pleasures and the politics of desire.

In his 'Salon' of 1765, Diderot enlivens his discussion of a contemporary painting – Greuze's portrait of his wife, whom Diderot claims to have fancied – by staging a little imaginary dialogue between 'himself' and 'Mlle Babuti', the woman who later became Mme Greuze. She ran a bookshop on the quai de Augustins in Paris. Diderot, he tells us, entered it one day and asked for the *Tales* of La Fontaine (not his *Fables*, but a much more licentious volume, filled with satirical portraits of boozy monks and wanton nuns), and the *Satyricon* of Petronius, an equally bawdy work. Then, hesitantly, he asked for what was obviously an even more risqué publication, one that he could barely bring himself to name: *The Nun in her Chemise*. 'How dare you, Monsieur! Does anyone have… does anyone read that kind of filth?' she replied. 'Oh, er… I see, it's filth is it? That I didn't know…'

A few days later he passed by the bookshop and she was smiling, and he smiled back.

(He may or may not have actually read the work: many have seen its influence on his own more tragic story of cloistered and closeted sex, *The Nun*. But let's leave that as a secret between him and Mlle Babuti.)

Theology

On 4 June 2012, the Vatican's Congregation for the Doctrine of the Faith issued a statement severely criticising Sister Margaret A. Farley for her book *Just Love: A Framework for Christian Sexual Ethics*, published back in 2006. Farley, a member of the Sisters of Mercy of America, is a distinguished moral theologian who was Gilbert L. Stark Professor of Christian Ethics at Yale Divinity School. Her book suggested that same-sex unions 'can [...] be important in transforming the hatred, rejection, and stigmatization of gays and lesbians'; that same-sex relationships could be justified as much as their heterosexual equivalent; that divorce could be reasonable option for couples who have drifted irreparably apart; and that, in her words, female masturbation 'usually does not raise any moral questions at all'. Many woman have found 'great good in self-pleasuring – perhaps especially in the discovery of their own possibilities for pleasure – something many had not experienced or even known about in their ordinary sexual relations with husbands or lovers'. The Vatican's response was a fairly standard re-statement of the teachings of the magisterium: homosexual acts are 'acts of grave depravity', 'intrinsically disordered' (i.e. not in harmony with God's designs for an ordered world), and 'contrary to the natural law'. Divorce could not be an option since marriage is a sacrament that, basically, cannot be dissolved. In short, 'The deliberate use of the sexual faculty, for whatever reason, outside of marriage is essentially contrary to its purpose.'

Venus in the Cloister begins with a scene of female masturbation and proceeds to explore same-sex relationships, specifically those between nuns. It does not mention divorce, still a barely conceivable option given that it depicts the world of late-seventeenth and early-eighteenth century France. But the acts on which it dwells all involve what the Vatican would recognize as 'the deliberate use of the sexual faculty [...] outside marriage'.

The Abbé du Prat brings his own insights to bear on this serious, contemporary, and political debate.

Translation

Some of the translators of the work have led interesting lives. Robert Samber (1682–1745) produced his version of *Venus in the Cloister* in 1724, though he was not named on the title page: the translation was simply ascribed to 'a man of honour'. The printer, Edmund Curll, although also not named on the title page, was duly prosecuted for obscenity, and convicted. For publishing *Venus in the Cloister* and two other books that were deemed to 'encourage vice and immorality', he was fined seventy marks and pilloried for an hour at Charing Cross.

French, the most erotic of languages (God's own, some have said) does not lend itself to translation. This is especially true of a work like *Venus in the Cloister*, where the syntactic poise of the original tends to come across as starchy formality, and the sensual throb of the source language as coy and vulgar. The nuns speak quite a high, classical French, but occasionally dally with something a little more vernacular: my nuns, generally decorous even when aroused, sometimes drop into the language of a chick-flick, and mix archaic and modern registers, for Venus loves anachronisms and the translator needs his own bit of *badinage*. I am not, I must confess, swayed by the translation theorists who dwell on the erotics of translation, unless it is an erotics of longing, in other words, an erotics *tout court* – so perhaps they are right after all. But still... the sighs, the languor, the *ah*s and *oh*s, the *tendresse*, the ache of the flesh, *mon cher coeur, tout en feu, je suis perdue...*

all is lost. Irrespective of the original language, you can't translate pornography, where it's really the words that are making love – or, to put it rather more sourly, there's something a bit pornographic about all translation: it isn't as good as the real thing, and is surely only ever meant to be a second-best, a way of getting you in the mood, a stage you'll grow out of: in short (or long), a glass dildo (see p. 39 below).

For real 'ecstatic intromission' (p. 38), the original text is avail-able in a cheap paperback (Paris: Librio, 2000), or in an excellent scholarly edition edited by Jean Sgard (*La Religieuse en chemise et le Cochon mitré*, Saint-Étienne, 2009 – it is from Sgard that I have derived almost all the historical details in this introduction). From *Venus* to *Vénus*: this is how the reader should progress – from a mere sex aid (a bit like a blow-up doll) to the real thing.

Venus in the Cloister

or

The Nun in a Chemise

Curious Conversations

TO MADAME D.L.R.
Most worthy Abbess of Beaulieu

Madame,

As it would be difficult for me not to carry out what you have stated that you desire, I did not long deliberate over the prayer you uttered to me, urging me to put in written form as soon as possible the sweet conversations in which your community has so zestfully participated. I promised to perform this gallant enterprise too solemnly to wish to decline the request now, and to excuse myself from this task on the grounds that it is difficult to restore to voice and action the lovely fire that so animated them. I do not know whether I will have fulfilled my duty and your hopes; the exercise of two or three mornings will reveal the truth of the matter to you, and will show you that, if I do not have a great deal of eloquence, I at least have enough memory to relate faithfully the greater part of what happened. I so much held your satisfaction before my eyes while composing this work that I have passed over, with indifference, all the reasons that should have kept me from it; only the fear that it might fall into other hands than yours made me postpone sending it to you for a while, and I myself would bear it to you, if my current affairs permitted, rather than entrusting to the hazards of the post, or of a messenger, such an important parcel. For, in all good faith, what embarrassment would ensue, for you and for me, if such secret conversations were to be made public! And if actions that do not incur blame merely because nobody knows of them were to comprise a new object of criticism, and furnish weapons to all those who would like to attack us! What posture and what countenance could our lovely nun keep, if misfortune exposed her, in her chemise, to the gaze of all curious folk? What opprobrium, what shame, what confusion! All these considerations weigh heavily; but you expressed the desire to be obeyed, and you treated as flimsy and timid excuses what are in fact sure and solid reasons.

Whatever happens, I wash my hands of it: and to leave seriousness aside for a moment, I can tell you that I have nothing to fear for Sister Agnès, even if an evil destiny were to put its hand to the business, since the depiction I give of her in my writings represents her only in the most exact conformity with all her own wishes. For, after all, beginning with *poverty*, can one be in a greater state of detachment from the good things of this world, than to strip oneself willingly of them, right down to one's *chemise*? Can one, in one's words and in one's actions, show the beauty *of chastity* as glowing any more than it does when it takes as its rule *nature most pure*? Finally, if we wish to prove her total *obedience*, it will be acknowledged that she is more docile than any of your novices.

This, Madame, is a long letter for a small work, and a big door for a poor house. Never mind; I prefer to sin against a few rules than to feel hampered in writing to you. Pass on to your most intimate lady friends, and mine as well, what you judge it right for them to know. And believe that I am without reserve,

Madame,
Your most obedient and most affectionate Servant,

THE ABBÉ DU PRAT

FIRST CONVERSATION
SISTER AGNÈS, SISTER ANGÉLIQUE

AGNÈS – Oh God! Sister Angélique, do not come into my room;
I am not decent right now. Do you think anyone should be
caught in my state? I really did think I had closed the door.

ANGÉLIQUE – Ah, calm down, dear; why all the alarm? What
a disaster – finding you in the middle of changing your chemise, or doing something better! When we girls are friends,
we really should not have anything at all to hide from one
another. Sit on your bed as you were, I will go and shut the
door behind us.

AGNÈS – I can assure you, Sister – I would die of shame if anyone else had caught me looking like this; but I am sure you
have a great deal of affection for me, which is why I do not
have any reason to be scared of you – whatever you might
have seen.

ANGÉLIQUE – You are quite right, my child; and even if I did
not have for you all the tenderness that a heart can feel, your
mind ought still to be at rest as far as *that* goes. I have been
a nun for seven years; I entered the cloister at thirteen, and
I can say that, so far, I have not made any enemies through
bad behaviour. I have always loathed spiteful gossip, and
I follow my heart's inclination most when I am doing a
favour to some fellow nuns. That is how I have won the
affection of most of them, especially that of our Superior,
which comes in quite useful from time to time.

AGNÈS – I know: and I am often amazed at how you have even
managed to handle nuns of different factions. One must
doubtless have as much skill and wit as you to win over
such persons. Personally, I have always given free rein to my
affections, and have never bothered to make an effort to gain

the friendship of those for whom I had no innate feelings. That is the weakness of my guiding spirit: an enemy of all constraint, and intent on acting with perfect freedom.

ANGÉLIQUE – Yes, it is so sweet to allow ourselves to be led to the purity and innocence of nature by following only the inclinations that she bestows on us; but honour and ambition have come to disturb the repose of the cloisters, and they oblige the girls who enter here to share themselves around, so that they often do out of prudence what they cannot do out of inclination.

AGNÈS – But that means that a countless number who think they are mistresses of your heart possess only its outward show, and that all your protestations of affection often assure them that they possess a treasure which in fact they do not. I have to confess that I would dread being one of that number, and falling victim to your schemes.

ANGÉLIQUE – Ah, my dear, that is really rather insulting! Dissimulation has no part in friendships as strong as ours. I belong to you alone; and even if nature had ensured that I was born from the same blood as you, she would not have given me feelings any more tender than those which I feel. Come into my arms, so that our hearts may speak to each other in the midst of our kisses.

AGNÈS – My God! How tightly you are hugging me! Had you not noticed that I am wearing nothing under this chemise? Oh, you are setting me on fire!

ANGÉLIQUE – Ah, how flushed you look now! It makes your beauty shine even more brightly! Oh, that fire gleaming in your eyes – it makes you so adorable! How can such an accomplished girl as you live in such retirement? No, no, my child, I have decided to divulge to you my most secret habits, and give you a perfect idea of the way a wise nun will behave. I do not mean the austere, over-punctilious wisdom whose only nourishment is fasting, and whose only clothing is prickly hair shirts; there is a less barbaric wisdom that all enlightened persons profess to follow, and which rather chimes in with your amorous propensities.

AGNÈS – My amorous propensities? Well, my face must give a very misleading impression, or you do not really know how to read it. There is nothing that affects me less than the passion of love, and during the three years since I took the veil, it has not given me the least disquiet.

ANGÉLIQUE – I very much doubt that – and I think that if you were to talk about it more sincerely, you would admit that everything I have said is quite true. Do you really think that a sixteen-year-old girl, with such a sharp mind and such an attractive physique as yours, is supposed to be frigid and insensible? No, that I *cannot* believe: all your most unself-conscious little actions have convinced me of the contrary, and that *je ne sais quoi* that I have spotted through your key-hole makes me sure that you are putting it all on.

AGNÈS – Oh God! I am done for!

ANGÉLIQUE – You are really not being very sensible. Go on, tell me what you have to fear from me, and if you have anything to worry about from a friend? I told you this only because I intend to tell you quite a few more secrets about me. Honestly, they are just silly little things! Even the most over-punctilious nuns indulge in them. In the language of the cloister, they are called: *the amusement of the young, and the pastime of the old*.

AGNÈS – But... well, what exactly have you noticed?

ANGÉLIQUE – Oh, stop putting on such an act! You know perfectly well that love banishes all fear, and that if we both want to live in the perfect intimacy that I desire, you must not conceal anything from me, and I must not have anything to hide from you. Kiss me, my sweetheart. In the state you are in, you could do with a good whipping to punish you for failing to reciprocate the friendship that people show to you. Oh God! What a plump little body! And a lovely shape to go with it! Allow me…

AGNÈS – Oh, please! Leave me alone; I cannot get over my shock – tell me honestly: what have you seen?

ANGÉLIQUE – You know perfectly well what I have seen, do you not, you stupid girl? I have seen you carrying out an activity in which I can help you myself, if you like – *my* hand will unhesitatingly perform the office that *your* hand was charitably performing for another part of your body. *That* is the great crime which I have discovered, which Mme the Abbess D.L.R. practises, as she says, in her most innocent pastimes, which the Prioress does not disdain, and which the Novice Mistress calls *ecstatic intromission*. You would never have believed that such holy souls were capable of performing such profane exercises. Their outward demeanour has deceived you; and that outward show of sanctity, which they know how to assume so opportunely, has led you to believe that they were living in their bodies as if they were composed of spirit alone. Ah, my child! I shall teach you so many things of which you are ignorant, if you will just trust me a little, and tell me what your state of mind and conscience is at present! After that, I want you to be my confessor; I will be your penitent, and I assure you that you will see my heart laid as bare as if you yourself could sense its subtlest movements.

AGNÈS – After so many words, I do not think I can possibly doubt your sincerity; that is why, not only will I tell you all that you wish to know about me, but I will even pleasure myself by communicating to you my most secret thoughts and actions. It will be a general confession, and I know that you have no intention of taking advantage of it; rather, my confidential sharing of it with you will serve merely to unite us one to the other in the closest and most indissoluble bond.

ANGÉLIQUE – There is no doubt about *that*, my dearest, and you will subsequently realise that there is nothing sweeter in this world than a real friend who can be the depositary of our secrets, of our thoughts, and even of our afflictions. Ah, what a relief it is to open one's heart on such occasions! So tell me everything, my darling; I will sit on your bed beside you; you do not need to get dressed, the warm weather means you can stay just as you are; I think you look even lovelier, and that, as you approach the state in which nature gave birth to you, your charms and your beauty increase. Put your arms round me, my dear Agnès, before you begin, and with your kisses confirm the mutual protestations of eternal love that we have exchanged. Ah, how pure and innocent are these kisses! Ah, how filled with tenderness and sweetness! Ah, how they flood me with pleasure! Let us rest for a moment, my little heart, I am all aflame, and with your caresses you are bringing me to the last extremity. Oh God! How powerful is love! And whatever will happen to me, if mere kisses transport me and arouse me so intensely?

AGNÈS – Ah, how difficult it is to keep within the limits of our duty, when we give rein even just a little to this passion! Would you believe it, Angélique? These sweet little caresses, which, basically, are nothing at all, have had the most wonderful effect on me! Ah! Ah! Ah! Give me time to breathe; I feel as if my heart were suffocating right now! Ah, these sighs are such a relief! I am starting to feel a new affection for you, more tender and more intense than before! I do not know why – can mere kisses throw a soul into such disarray? Admittedly, you are very skilful in your caresses, and your whole manner is extraordinarily alluring; you have so captivated me that I now belong more to you than to myself. I even feel that the excess of the satisfaction that I have enjoyed might have been due to a touch of something that ought to make me think of my conscience; and that would really annoy me, since, when I have to tell my confessor about this kind of thing, I die of shame and do not know where to start. Ah, God! How weak we are, and how vain our efforts to surmount the least sallies and most tentative attacks of a corrupt nature!

Angélique – That is just what I was expecting you to say: I know you have always been rather over-punctilious on many subjects, and that a certain tenderness of conscience has caused you considerable pain. That is the result of falling into the hands of an uncouth, ignorant spiritual director. Personally, I can tell you that I was instructed by a know-ledgeable man on how I should behave if I wanted to live happy all my life long, though without doing anything which could shock the view of a regular religious community, or which might be directly opposed to God's command-ments.

Agnès – I shall be much obliged, Sister Angélique, if you would give me a perfect idea of such proper behaviour; believe me, I am entirely disposed to listen and to be swayed by your arguments, if I cannot destroy them by stronger arguments. The promise that I had made you to lay myself bare to you will be all the more closely kept, since, imperceptibly, in the replies which I will interject into our conversation, you will realise what kind of upbringing I was given, and you will be able to judge, from the sincere and full confession I make, of the good or bad path I will follow.

ANGÉLIQUE – My child, you may well be surprised by the lessons I am going to give you, and you will be amazed to hear a girl of nineteen or twenty passing herself off as knowledgeable and able to penetrate into the most hidden secrets of religious politics. Do not imagine, my dear, that a spirit of vain glory inspires my words: no, I am aware that I was even less enlightened than you at your age, and that everything I have learned came after a period of extreme ignorance; but I also have to admit that I could rightfully be accused of stupidity, if the care that several great man have taken in educating me had not borne any fruit, and if the knowledge of several languages they gave me had not enabled me to make some progress by reading good books.

AGNÈS – My dear Angélique, do begin your instruction, I beg you; I am languishing with impatience to hear you. You have never had a pupil more attentive than I to follow all you have to say.

ANGÉLIQUE – Since we were not born of a sex able to pass any laws, we must obey those laws which we have found in place, and follow, as known truths, many things which of themselves frequently pass as mere opinions. I thus hope, my child, to confirm you in your sense that there is a just and merciful God who requires our homage and who, with the same mouth that forbids us to do evil, commands us to practise good. But since not all people agree on what is to be called good or evil, and since countless actions which we are told to shun are accepted and approved by our neighbours, I will teach you in a few words what a Reverend Jesuit Father, who has a particular affection for me, told me when he was trying to broaden my mind and make it capable of these present speculations.

'Since all your happiness, my dear Angélique,' (this is how he spoke) 'depends on a perfect understanding of the religious state that you have embraced, I will depict it to you frankly and provide you with the means of living in your solitude without any anxiety or sorrow that might ensue on your making this commitment. In order to proceed with method in the instruction I shall give you, you need to realise that religion (by this I mean all the monastic orders) is composed of two bodies, one of which is purely heavenly and supernatural, and the other earthly and corruptible, being merely the invention of men; the one is political, and the other mystical in relation to Jesus Christ, who is the sole head of the true Church. The one is permanent, since it consists of the word of God which is immutable and eternal, and the other is subject to countless changes, since it depends on the word of men, which is finite and fallible. Given this, we must separate these two bodies, and discern fairly between them, if we are to discover what our true obligations are. It is no small difficulty to tell them apart. Politics, as the weaker part, has so united itself with the other, stronger part, that everything is now in an almost complete muddle, and the voice of men confused with the voice of God. It is from this confusion that illusions, scruples, constraints, and those pangs of conscience that sometimes bring a poor soul to despair have all arisen, and this yoke, which should be light and easy to bear, has, by being imposed by men, become heavy, burdensome and unbearable for many.

'In such deep darkness, when all things have so obviously changed their real shape, we need to focus on the trunk of the tree without worrying about taking in all its branches and twigs. We need to content ourselves with obeying the precepts of the sovereign Legislator, and we can hold it as certain that all those works of supererogation which men's voices wish to enjoin on us should not cause us a moment's disquiet. We should, while obeying the God who commands us, see whether his will is written by his own fingers, whether it emerges from his son's mouth, or whether it comes merely from the mouth of the people. Thus, Sister Angélique can, without scruple, loosen her chains, brighten her solitude, and, endowing all her actions with gaiety, be sociable with the outside world. She can' – he continued – 'dispense, insofar as is prudent, with the execution of that whole hotchpotch of vows and promises that she has made, indiscreetly, while in the hands of men, and return to the same rights that she enjoyed before committing herself to religious life, following her earliest obligations alone.

'So much,' he continued, 'for inner peace; as for outward appearances, you cannot, without sinning against prudence, be dispensed from appearing to conform with the laws, customs and way of life to which you subjected yourself when you entered the cloister. You must even appear zealous and fervent in the most unpleasant exercises, if any measure of renown or honour depends on these occupations; you can decorate your room with hair shirts and scourges, and put on a display of devoutness which will mean that you merit as much as the girl who indiscreetly lacerates her body with them.'

AGNÈS – Ah, how delighted I am to hear that! The extreme pleasure I was taking in your words stopped me from interrupting you, and the liberty of conscience that your words are starting to restore to me frees me from the almost countless pains that were tormenting me. But carry on, I beg you, and tell me what it was that politics intended by establishing so many orders, whose rules and constitutions are so rigorous.

ANGÉLIQUE – We can think about the two labourers who participated in the foundation of all monasteries, namely the founder, and politics. The intention of the first was often pure, holy, and far removed from all the designs of the second. And, with nothing other than saving souls in mind, the founder put forward rules and ways of life that he thought necessary, or at least useful for his spiritual progress as well as his neighbour's. That is how the deserts became peopled, and the cloisters were built. The zeal of one man inspired many others, and their main occupation was to sing continually the praises of the true God; their pious exercises thus drew whole companies to join them and form one single body. I am here talking about what happened in the first centuries; we need to adopt a different point of view for the rest, and not imagine that this primitive innocence and this splendid piety were long maintained, or were inherited by those we see at present.

Politics, which can suffer no defects in a State, saw the number of these recluses increasing, and the disorder of the unregulated lives they were leading; it was thus obliged to intervene, banishing some of them and abolishing from the constitutions of other communities those elements that it did not think necessary to the common interest. It would indeed have wished to rid itself entirely of those leeches who, in the most appalling sloth and laziness, grew fat on the labour of the poor; but the shield of religion by which they were protected, and the minds of the common people which they had already bewitched, made another stratagem necessary if these various companies were not to be completely useless to the commonwealth.

So politics regarded all of these religious houses as common pits into which it could discharge its superfluities; it uses them for the relief of families which their great number of children would render poor and indigent if they did not have places to which they could send them away. And, so that their seclusion would be permanent, politics invented vows by which it claims to bind us and attach us indissolubly to the state which it forces us to embrace; it even makes us renounce the rights which nature has given us, and removes us so far from the world that we no longer form part of it. Do you follow all this?

AGNÈS – Yes, but how does it come about that this accursed politics, which makes us slaves where we were free, more greatly approves of rules that are altogether harsh and austere, than of those that are less rigorous?

ANGÉLIQUE – For this reason: politics regards monks and nuns as limbs cut off from its body, separate parts whose life does not seem of particular use for anything, but is rather a danger to the public. And as it would seem inhumane to rid itself of them openly, it uses stratagems and, on the pretext of piety, it forces these poor victims to turn a sacrificial knife upon themselves, and to burden themselves with so many fasts, penances and mortifications that those innocent men and women finally succumb and, by dying, give way to others who are bound to be just as wretched, unless they are more enlightened. In this way, the father is often the executioner of his children, sacrificing them unthinkingly to politics, when he believes he is simply offering them to God.

AGNÈS – Ah! The pitiful effect of a detestable system of government! You are restoring me to life, dear Angélique, as you gently reason me away from the highroad I was following. Few people have resorted more than I did to all the harshest mortifications. I flogged myself mercilessly, in my struggle against what were often the innocent impulses of nature –

which my spiritual director viewed as horrible profligacy. Ah, to think how deceived I was! It was doubtless thanks to this cruel maxim that the moderate religious orders are scorned, and the fiercely demanding orders are praised and exalted to the heavens. Oh God! Can you really allow your name to be abused in the cause of such unjust executions, and can you really allow men to act as if they were you?

ANGÉLIQUE – Ah, my child, these exclamations show that you still lack light to see clearly and generally into the way things are! Let us leave it at that: your mind is not at present capable of any more delicate speculations. *Love God and your neighbour*, and believe that the whole law is included in those two commandments.

AGNÈS – What? Angélique, could you be content to leave me in a state of error?

ANGÉLIQUE – No, my sweetheart, you will be fully instructed, and I will place in your hands a book that will make you perfectly wise, and in which you will learn with ease the things that I can explain to you only confusedly.

AGNÈS – That will be enough. I have to confess that I found those words rather amusing: *common pits into which politics can discharge its superfluities*! In my view, it would not be possible to speak of it in baser, more humiliating terms.

ANGÉLIQUE – The expression is, admittedly, rather strong; but it is hardly more shocking than the words uttered by another man, who said that *monks and monkesses played the same part in the Church as cats and mice did in Noah's Ark*.

AGNÈS – You are right, and I admire the ease with which you find the right words; I would not have missed out, not for all that I hold most dear, on the opportunity my open door has given us of conversing together. Yes, I have fully grasped the meaning of all your words.

ANGÉLIQUE – Well, will you put them to good use? And will this lovely body, guiltless of any crime, still be treated like the most vile criminal in the world?

AGNÈS – No, I hope to make up to it for all the bad times I have given it; I ask its forgiveness, in particular for a harsh flogging that I imposed on it yesterday, on the advice of my confessor.

ANGÉLIQUE – Kiss me, my poor child; I am more touched by what you have to say than if I had suffered that flogging myself. That punishment must be the last inflicted on you; but... did you really hurt yourself?

AGNÈS – Alas, my zeal was indiscreet, and I believed that, the harder I lashed myself, the more merit I would have; my plumpness and my youthful body made me sensitive to the slightest blows: as a result, at the end of this fine exercise, my backside was inflamed; indeed, I might actually have broken the skin, since I was beside myself, belabouring it so fiercely.

ANGÉLIQUE – My darling, I will just *have* to have a look, and see what misguided fervour can do.

AGNÈS – Oh God! Must I suffer such a thing? So... are you really speaking seriously? I cannot endure it without shame. Oh! Oh!

ANGÉLIQUE – And what, then, is the use of everything I have been telling you, if a stupid sense of modesty still holds you back? What wrong can there be in your granting what I am asking?

AGNÈS – It is true, I am wrong, and there is nothing blame-worthy in your curiosity; satisfy it as you wish.

ANGÉLIQUE – Ah, so there it is, that lovely face that is always veiled! Kneel down on your couch and lower your head a little, so that I can examine the violence of your lashes. Ah,

17

good heavens, what a bright patchwork of colours! I could well imagine that I am seeing China taffeta, or even striped fabric from bygone days! One must have a great devotion to the *mystery of the Flagellation* to illuminate one's buttocks in such a manner.

AGNÈS – Well, have you done contemplating this poor injured innocent? Oh God, how you are pawing it! Leave it in peace, so that it may regain its former complexion and lose this hue so foreign to it. What? Are you kissing it?

ANGÉLIQUE – Do not resist, my child, I have the most compassionating soul in the world, and as it is a work of mercy to console the afflicted, I feel I can never caress them too tenderly if I am to acquit myself worthily of this duty. Ah! This part of your body has such a lovely shape! And how white and round it is – it dazzles the eyes! I have also set my eyes on another place that is no less a work of nature – I mean *nature herself*.

AGNÈS – Withdraw your hand, I beg you, from that spot, unless you wish to light a blaze there that would be difficult to extinguish. I must confess to you, I have a particular weakness: I am the most sensitive girl you could find, and what would not so much as stir others often throws me into complete disarray.

ANGÉLIQUE – What? So you are not as frigid as you wanted to convince me at the start of our conversation! And I think you will play your part just as well as any girl I know, once I have placed you in the hands of five or six good friars. And, while we are on the subject – if only the time for us to retire (as I am about to, in accordance with custom) could be postponed, so that I could be with you in the parlour! But never mind: I will console myself with your account of all that happens – I mean whether the *abbot* does better than the *friar*, whether the *Feuillant* outperforms the *Jesuit*, and, finally, whether the whole lot satisfy you with their *monking around*.

AGNÈS – Ah! How awkward I imagine I will be in that sort of conversation, and what a novice they will find me when it comes to amorous dallyings!

ANGÉLIQUE – Do not worry yourself; they know just how to treat everybody, and a quarter of an hour with them will make you wiser than all the precepts that you could hear from me in a week. Well now, cover your backside in case it catches cold. Ha! – it will have just another kiss from me… and another… and one more…

AGNÈS – You are *such* a tease! Do you think I would have put up with this nonsense unless I had known that no offence was involved?

ANGÉLIQUE – And if any offence *were* involved, I would be sinning at every moment, since I have been put in charge of all the girls who are pupils or boarders here and am thus obliged to inspect their rear annexes really rather frequently. Only yesterday I was giving a whipping to one – for my own satisfaction rather than for any wrong she had committed: I took a singular pleasure in gazing at her; she is really pretty, and thirteen years old already.

AGNÈS – I am filled with longing for a similar job as school mistress, so that I could enjoy myself in a similar way. It is an overpowering fantasy – indeed, I would be delighted to see in your person what you have been contemplating so attentively in my own.

ANGÉLIQUE – Alas! My child, your request comes as no surprise to me; we are all formed from the same dough. Look, I will adopt the same posture as you. Good: now lift my skirt and my chemise as high as you can.

19

AGNÈS – I am sorely tempted to reach for my whip, and use it in such a way that these two twin sisters have no reason to rebuke me.

ANGÉLIQUE – Ow! Ow! Ow! How you lay it on! I like this sort of game only when it is not violent. Pax! Faynights! If you were to be seized by another such attack of piety, I would be doomed. Oh God! That arm of yours can really swing! I am thinking about sharing my job with you… but you need to be a little more moderate.

AGNÈS – Oh, you really have no cause for complaint! That was not a tenth of the lashes that I received; I will let you off the rest, and save them for another time: I must make allowances for your lack of staying power. As you must know, that place becomes even more beautiful as a result: a certain fire that glows there infuses it with a bright vermilion glow more brilliant than all the red of Spain. Move a little closer to the window, so that, in the daylight, it will display all its beauties to me. Ah, it looks so lovely. I would never tire of gazing at it; I can see all that I wanted to, including even the thing just round the corner. Why are you covering that part with your hand?

ANGÉLIQUE – Alas! You can contemplate it just as much as everything else; even if there is anything wrong with such a way of passing the time, it does not hurt anyone and in no way disturbs public order.

AGNÈS – How could it disturb it? We are no longer part of that public. In any case, hidden misdeeds are half forgiven.

ANGÉLIQUE – You are right – for, if so many crimes (to speak in conformity with our rules) were committed in the world as are in our cloisters, the police would be obliged to correct such abuses and would put a stop to such lawlessness.

AGNÈS – I also believe that fathers and mothers would never allow their children to enter our houses, if they knew what dissoluteness prevails here.

ANGÉLIQUE – Of that there is no doubt; but since most of the misdeeds committed here are secret, and since dissimulation reigns more absolutely here than anywhere else, all those who live here do not even notice these failings, but themselves help to lure others in – and the particular interests of a family often prevail over many other considerations.

AGNÈS – The confessors and spiritual directors of cloisters have a particular talent for catching in their nets poor innocent girls who think they have found a treasure but merely fall into the trap.

ANGÉLIQUE – That is true, and I have experienced it in my own person. I had no inclination towards the religious life; I persistently opposed the reasons put forward by the people who urged me to adopt it, and I would never have entered this house unless a Jesuit, who at the time was in charge of this convent, had become involved: a family interest obliged my mother, who loved me tenderly, and who had always opposed this plan, to agree. I resisted for a long time, since I did not foresee that the Count de la Roche, my elder brother, by right of nobility and the customs of the country, would inherit almost all the family property, leaving six of us defenceless, apart from the support which he promised – and which, given his temperament, would clearly not amount to much. Finally he yielded ten thousand francs, or so he told me, from the amount he claimed, and four thousand were added, with the result that I brought a dowry of fourteen thousand pounds when I took my vows in this convent. But, to return to the deep designs of the man who gave me a place here, I can tell you that it was arranged that I would meet with him one evening after dinner when I had gone to pay a visit to one of my girl cousins who was a nun, and who was dying to see me dressed in a habit like hers.

AGNÈS – You mean Sister Victorie?

ANGÉLIQUE – Yes. So, when the three of us found ourselves in the same parlour – the Jesuit, Victorie and myself – we began with the compliments and civilities that are customary at a first interview. They were followed by a speech in which this loyalist touched on the vanities of the secular world, and the difficulty of finding salvation in it. His words greatly predisposed my soul to allow itself to be deceived. They were, however, the merest preparatory feints: he had many other subtle tricks to insinuate himself into my heart, and to lure me into sharing his sentiments. He repeatedly told me that he could see in my face the authentic characteristics of a religious soul: that he had a particular gift for forming a just discernment of such things, and that I could not, without insult to God (there were the words he used), devote to the world a beauty as perfect as mine.

AGNÈS – Not a bad way of going about it. What did you say in reply to all that?

ANGÉLIQUE – I began by opposing these first arguments with others – but he destroyed them with marvellous cunning. Victorie too helped to deceive me, and made me see religion in a rather favourable light, adroitly concealing everything that I might find off-putting in it. Finally, the Jesuit, who (as I have since learned) had made the conquest of many more reluctant girls, deployed his final efforts to ensure he conquered me. He succeeded thanks to his depiction of the world and the religious life, and he constrained me, by the force of his eloquence, to embrace his party with fervour.

AGNÈS – But… whatever did he say that could exercise such an absolute power over your mind?

ANGÉLIQUE – I cannot relate it to you in its entirety, since he kept me at the grille for three hours. I will merely say that he proved to me, by chains of reasoning which I found persuasive, that this was my vocation in which alone I could find salvation, that there was no safety for myself, nor any path outside this one; that the world was full of reefs and precipices, that the excesses of the religious life were worth more than the moderation of the worldly life, and that the repose and contemplation of the former were at one and the same time sweeter and more meritorious than all the activity and hustle-bustle of the latter; that it was in the cloisters alone that one could treat with God on familiar terms and that, in consequence, it was necessary to flee from the company of men if one was to become worthy of such a holy and lofty communication; for it was in these places that something of the ancient fervour of Christians was still maintained, and here the true image of the primitive Church could be found.

AGNÈS – No one could have spoken with more eloquence – or more cunning; for I notice that he did not utter a word about the rigours and austerities that might have filled you with alarm.

ANGÉLIQUE – You are wrong, he omitted nothing. But the pains and mortifications of which he spoke to me were seasoned with so much sweetness that I found they did not taste at all unpleasant. 'I will hide nothing from you,' he told me. 'These devout companies, whose number I hope you will increase, labour day and night, by their austerities and penances, to tame the pride and insolence of nature; they inflict a perpetual violence on their senses; although their souls do not die, they are separated from their bodies, and, holding pain and pleasure in equal contempt, they live as if they were made of spirit alone. And that is not all' – he continued in persuasive tones – 'for they rigorously sacrifice their freedom, they strip themselves of all their goods to enrich themselves with their hopes alone, and impose on themselves, by solemn vows, the necessity of a perpetual virtue.'

AGNÈS – This disciple of Loyola was a master orator: I would like to meet him.

ANGÉLIQUE – You know him well, and I will tell you a few particular details of his life that suggest he plays more than one role. But I need to end my story. 'Mademoiselle,' he continued, 'behold the many chains, the many rigours and mortifications that I am presenting you with; but – can you believe it? – those holy souls I was speaking of just now are proud of this yoke, they are vain of this servitude, and there is no harsh pain they endure that they do not consider to be a great reward; all their love, all their passion goes to the service of Jesus Christ; he alone sets them aflame, merely at a touch; he alone is the sole master of their hearts, and can ensure that their pains are followed by incredible joys and delights.'

AGNÈS – I suppose you were enchanted by this handsome talker?

ANGÉLIQUE – Yes, my child, the charlatan persuaded me; his words transformed me in an instant; they tugged me away from myself and led me ardently to seek what I had always persistently fled. I became the most punctilious woman in the world – and, since he had told me that I could not find salvation outside the cloister, I imagined that, before I entered it, I must have been surrounded by a great throng of devils. Since then, he himself has tried to put me back on the road of commonsense; he has given me the knowledge that could draw me out of the darkness into which he had thrown me, and it is thanks to his moral lessons that I owe all the repose and quietude of mind that I possess.

AGNÈS – So, tell me quickly, who is this character?

ANGÉLIQUE – It is Father de Raucourt.

AGNÈS – Oh God! That enchanter! I once went to make my confession to him, I took him to be the most devout man in the world: it is true that he knows to perfection the art of winning souls, and that he can persuade you of whatever he wishes. But I am not pleased with him, for he left me in the error in which he found me, and from which he could have saved me.

ANGÉLIQUE – Ah, he is too prudent to take such risks! He saw that you were in a state of extraordinary bigotry, in thrall to the most horrible scruples, and he knew that a girl cannot be led from one extremity to the other so easily. In addition, if a single saint were to enlighten all the blind, there would be no miracles for the others to perform – you understand? In other words, if you had had faith, you would have been cured, and if this wise director had recognised in you any disposition to follow his prescriptions, he would have served as your doctor.

AGNÈS – So I believe, but I am just as happy to be obliged to you for this service as to him. So, I beg you, tell me something of the life of this blessed man.

ANGÉLIQUE – I will happily do so, my sweetheart, so kiss me and embrace me fondly before I do. Ah… ah… that is so nice! Ah, how the beauty of your mouth and your eyes delights me; a single one of your kisses transports me more than I can express.

AGNÈS – Please begin. Ah, what a great kisser you are!

ANGÉLIQUE – I never weary of caressing a person I find lovable. Since you know Father de Raucourt, I do not need to tell you that he is the most intriguing, the most cunning and the wittiest man you could ever meet. I will merely point out that, when it comes to friendship, he is fastidious to the highest degree and that, since he thinks he is a man of some distinction, you must have a good number of qualities if you are to please him. The conquest of which he was proudest was the conquest he had made of a young nun from a convent in this town, Sister Virginie by name.

AGNÈS – I have heard her described as a consummate beauty, but I know nothing more about her.

ANGÉLIQUE – She is the most beautiful girl you could ever come across, if the portrait of her that her gallant has shown me is faithful. As for wit, she is as well endowed with it as she could have hoped; she is playful; she plays several instruments, and sings with a charm that could ravish your heart away. Our Jesuit had already acquired her for himself several months ago, and the two of them were enjoying that sweet tranquillity that comprises all the happiness of lovers, when jealousy upset everything, as you are about to hear.

In that same convent there was a nun towards whom the Father had shown some friendship, and to whom he had consequently paid several visits: he had even received from her several favours that would tie down any man capable of fidelity – but Virginie's dazzling beauty won his heart over. He detached himself, within, from that first habit, giving the poor girl nothing more than the outward signs and appearances of true love. She soon noticed this change, and saw clearly that she was sharing his affection with another. However, she concealed her grief, and – seeing that she was up against a rival who surpassed her on every score – she decided not to try and attack her, but swore instead to destroy the man who had scorned her.

In order to carry out her plans more easily, she studied the hours and minutes that Virginie devoted to the entertainment of this lover priest; and, as she had learned from experience that he was not satisfied with mere words or superficial favours, she correctly thought that she would be able to catch them at certain exercises a knowledge of which would make her the mistress of the fate of her unfaithful swain. It was some time before she could discover anything convincing enough to expose them: indeed, on two or three occasions she spotted that unhappy Father warming his hand on Virginie's breast; she saw them exchanging a few kisses of incredible ardour; but, to her way of thinking, these were the merest bagatelles; and since she knew that, in the cloisters, such actions counted as simple peccadilloes easily washed away by holy water, she kept her silence, while waiting for a better opportunity to speak.

AGNÈS – Ah, how I fear for poor Virginie!

ANGÉLIQUE – Our lovers, who had no inkling of the ambush being prepared for them, took no measures to protect themselves. They saw each other two or three times a week, and wrote letters to each other when prudence obliged them to separate for a while for fear of giving rise to gossip. The Father's letters, with their intense and tender expressions, ensured that Virginie was entirely his. He went to see her after a week's absence, and noted from her eyes and the look on her face that he would now be able to have from her what she had always previously refused him. However, her rival was not being lazy; for, having reached an understanding with the Mother Janitor, she had learned of the Jesuit's arrival and, doubting not that, after such a long period apart, they would indulge in intimacies of the kind she would have preferred for herself, she went off, smouldering with jealousy, to a place near the parlour where, by means of a small opening that she made, she could observe even the slightest movements of those who were talking together there, and listen in on their most secret conversations.

AGNÈS – At this point, my fears are renewed. Ah, how I hate that prying woman for so maliciously disturbing the repose of two unhappy lovers!

ANGÉLIQUE – So that the eyewitness account she intended to give of what she saw would be heard and believed, she took with her another nun who would be able to bear witness with her. So the two of them took up their positions in the place I mentioned, and saw our two lovers conversing more in looks and sighs than in words. They were squeezing each other's hands and gazing languorously at one another, exchanging a few tender words that came more from their hearts than from their lips. This amorous contemplation was followed by the opening of a little square window that was near the middle of the grille, and was used for passing through the parcels of any size that were given as presents to the nuns. It was now that Virginie received and gave a thousand kisses, but with such transports of delight, with such unexpected sallies, that the act of love itself would not have increased their ardour. 'Ah, my dear Virginie!' began our man, inflamed with passion, 'Do you really want us to go no further? Alas, how little love you show in return to those who love you, and how well you indulge in the art of tormenting them!'

'And how,' replied our vestal virgin, 'can I make you a present of anything else, after giving you my heart? Ah, how tyrannical is your love! I know what you desire; I even know that I was weak enough to lead you to hope for it; but I am aware that it is all the wealth and riches that I have, and that I can grant it to you only if I reduce myself to poverty. Can we not, while remaining within our current terms, spend sweet times together, and enjoy pleasures that are all the more perfect in that they are pure and innocent? If your happiness, as you tell me, depends only on the loss of what I hold most dear, you can be happy only once, and I will always be wretched, since it is a thing that cannot be recovered in order to be lost again. Believe me, let us love one another as a brother loves a sister, and let us give to this love all the liberties it can imagine for itself, with the exception of just one.'

AGNÈS – And did the Jesuit not reply to all that?

ANGÉLIQUE – No; throughout this speech of hers he said nothing; but, propping up his head on one hand, he gazed with eyes full of languor at the woman speaking to him. After which, taking her hand across the grille, he said to her, in poignant tones, 'So we need to change tack, and not love as before. Can you do so, Virginie? For my part, I cannot diminish any part of my love: the rules you have just laid down for me cannot be accepted by any true lover.' Then he so exaggerated to her, with his fervent expressions, the excess of his ardour that he completely disconcerted her and drew from her a spoken promise that she would grant to him, within a few days, that which alone would make him perfectly happy. He then made her come closer to the grille and, having made her climb onto a high chair, he enjoined her to allow him to satisfy his view at least, since any other liberty was forbidden him. After some resistance she obeyed, and gave him time to see and fondle the places dedicated to chastity and self-control. She, for her part, also wished to content her eyes, being equally curious; the Jesuit, who was not insensible, easily found the means to do so, and she obtained from him what she desired, with greater ease than she had granted him a view of her. This was the fateful moment for both of them, and the moment that our two spies had been longing for. They contemplated, with the most intense satisfaction, the loveliest parts of their companion's naked body, as the Jesuit uncovered them and fondled them, filled with the transports of a lover, almost beside himself. They gazed now at one part and now at another, as the officious Father turned his lover round and made her change posture; as a result, as he was staring at her front parts, he exposed her backside to their view, since her skirt was on both sides raised up to her belt.

AGNÈS – It is just as if I were present at this spectacle – you are giving me such a clear and vivid account of it.

ANGÉLIQUE – Finally, they brought their frolics to an end, and our two sisters withdrew, intent on putting a stop to these ill-conducted amours and preventing Virginie's promise from being put into effect. That poor innocent girl was particularly lucky, for the nun whom Virginie's rival had persuaded to observe these events with her had a most tender friendship for the girl and tried to find some cunning way of destroying the Jesuit without harming the girl she cherished. She told Virginie what she knew about her, and assured her that she would do nothing to damage her good name, provided that she promise to break off completely with the priest and in future have not the slightest communication with him. Virginie, filled with shame at what she was being told, agreed to do all that was desired, demanding merely that the Jesuit's reputation not be ruined, since it was impossible to hurt one of them without harming the other. She protested that she did not want to see him, and that the letter she was about to write telling him not to return would be the last he ever received from her. These conditions were accepted by both women, albeit reluctantly. They embraced Virginie, with whom they had fallen in love, and told her as they left that they wished to fill the Father's place and strike up a close friendship with her.

Agnès – She had got off lightly. I think she owed this indulgence to her beauty and her other qualities, that doubtless made her lovable even to the woman who hated her.

Angélique – We have still not reached the end of our story. So Virginie promptly wrote to Father de Raucourt, and informed him in her letter of everything that had happened and of the conditions to which she had agreed to save his honour and her own. She pointed out the danger to which he would expose himself if he came back to see her, and told him that she would not even be able to receive his letters if he did not use some clever ruse to avoid interception. She concluded with protestations of her constant love, safe from all the fiercest attacks of jealousy, and gave him hope that time might disperse the storm now threatening them and make them happier than before. I do not need to say how surprised the Father was when he received this letter and read it. It was a thunderbolt from the blue. He saw that there was little point in replying, and that he would have to yield to the misfortune which had struck his good fortune just as he was on the point of enjoying it.

Three weeks of this widowed state had already passed when Virginie, growing bored with her solitude, found an unbelievably cunning way of learning how her lover was and informing him about herself. She pretended that she had forgotten to send Father de Raucourt a square bonnet that he had asked her to make at the time of their past familiarities. Her rival told her that she needed to deliver it to him by hand and that she would have it kept by the *tourière*.[1] This was done. The messenger was told what she was to say. She acquitted herself of her task punctiliously, and the Jesuit, having received the bonnet, asked her to wait for a while in the church, so that he would have time to think about what he saw. After a few moments' reflection, he guessed what stratagem was being employed, made a hole in part of the bonnet, and there found a letter from Virginie; without reading it too carefully, he immediately wrote a reply, which he put into the same place, then sealed it as best he could with two or three stitches. He went back to the *tourière*, whom he asked to take the bonnet back as it needed altering – it was much too tight for him, and he had tried it on several men in the house, so as to spare its maker the trouble it would take her to widen it, but he had not found any Father on whose head it fitted. In any case, he was very obliged to her for the patience she had shown in waiting so long. The good sister replied with a bow to the Father's civilities and took the square bonnet back to the convent; following the orders of the woman who had sent it, she handed it over to Virginie, who was delighted to learn the news of the man she loved, and the cunning plan's success.

AGNÈS – One has to admit that love is most inventive!

ANGÉLIQUE – This commerce lasted over a month. There was always some alteration that needed to be done to that venerable bonnet; every three days, it had to be taken to the Jesuit college and then returned to the convent. However, nobody so much as imagined that there was anything mysterious in such a thing; nobody paid it any attention, and they could have continued to use this postman bonnet, had it not been for an accident that led to its being discharged.

Agnès – Oh God! I imagine that the *tourière* fathomed the mystery.

Angélique – No, you are wrong. It came about when, one fast day, the Jesuits' porter was in a bad mood, perhaps because he had not enjoyed his orange marmalade in the usual way; the *tourière*, who had countless tasks to do, including delivering the bonnet, rang two or three times at the door of the college to pass on her message as quickly as possible. This good brother left the garden where he was, and arrived out of breath, thinking that it must be some bishop or archbishop, or some other dignitary, who had rung with such magisterial force. He was highly surprised to see the good sister, who had nothing else to tell him but to hand the square bonnet to Father de Raucourt. The boorish fellow, tired to death of so many unpleasant visits, flew into a rage and said that this bonnet was going to and fro rather too frequently and that he would place it in the safekeeping of a man who would give him a little peace and quiet. The *tourière*, apologising as best as she could, withdrew; the rector, who was waiting for a companion in the porter's lodge so that he could go out, had overheard this dialogue; he called over the brother and asked what the subject of the dispute was, and why he was treating people who had business with the residents of the house so rudely. The brother responded to his superior's rebuke by telling him everything he suspected about this bonnet, assured him that it had already travelled back and forth between the college and the nunnery nearly twenty times, and there was doubtless some secret stratagem hidden in this strange behaviour. If it pleased His Reverence, he would examine this item, which he supposed to be some contraband: whereupon he did so, and with a pair of scissors he brought into the light of day the fifteenth *child of the square bonnet* that had come directly from Sister Virginie.

AGNÈS – Oh God! How difficult it is for people to be safe when an evil destiny pursues them and has sworn to destroy them! What was the result of all this?

ANGÉLIQUE – What happened was that the Father was exiled to another province, and poor Virginie was given the mortification of a few penances; and this is the origin of the proverb *that there is a good deal of malice under the square bonnet of a Jesuit.*

AGNÈS – Ah, it was for her alone that I was fearful! But tell me how this came to the Prioress's knowledge.

ANGÉLIQUE – It would take too long to dwell on this subject now. In the first conversation after my retreat, I will tell you more about it. I will show you two of the children of the square bonnet and tell you of the fate that befell their father and mother. Just remember now, my dearest, that I will be spending the next week to ten days in great sadness, since I will be unable to have the slightest conversation with you. I will write to three of my good friends so they will visit you during this time: they are an Abbot, a Feuillant, and a Capuchin.

AGNÈS – Oh God, what a motley crew! What on earth do you expect me to do with all those people whom I do not even know?

ANGÉLIQUE – You merely have to be obedient: they will teach you your duty well enough, so that you will satisfy them and content yourself. Look, here is a book that I will lend you; make good use of it: it will instruct you of many things, and will give your spirit all the quietude that you could wish for.

Kiss me, my dear child, for all the time I must be without you. Ah, with what pleasure I would spend my retreat if the spiritual director I have were as lovable and docile as you are! Farewell, my sweetheart, get dressed, keep our friendship completely secret and prepare to tell me of all your pastimes when I have emerged from the exercises of my retreat.

SECOND CONVERSATION
SISTER ANGÉLIQUE, SISTER AGNÈS

ANGÉLIQUE – Ah, God be praised! I can breathe again! I have never been so overburdened with devotions, mysteries and indulgences as since I left you. Ah, how all these superstitions disgust me! How are you? Do you not have anything to say to me? Why are you laughing?

AGNÈS – I am filled with shame at appearing before you. I imagine you already know the least little detail of what has been said and done during your absence?

ANGÉLIQUE – And from whom could I have learned it? You mock me. Come into my room, and prepare to make me a faithful narration of these things. As for me, I have just escaped from the hands of a savage who would have plunged anyone with a different cast of mind into despair: I mean my spiritual director; he is the harshest and most ignorant man you could imagine. I think he ensured that I obtained all the indulgences and pardons ever granted by the popes, from Gregory the Great to Innocent XI. If I had believed him, my whole body would have bled, thanks to the lashes which he ordered me to apply to it: not because I displayed much malice in the confessions he heard me making, but because he imagines that, in order to be on the road to paradise, you have to be as dry, skinny and emaciated as he is, and that if you are just a little bit agreeable and have just a little flesh on your bones, you deserve every kind of penance. So you can guess how I spent my time, and judge whether or not I have grounds for feeling vexed.

AGNÈS – For my part, I have to say that you gave me spiritual directors who wore me out almost as much as yours did you. I do not know if I obtained any indulgences from them, but I am certain that, in order to obtain them, many people do far less than we have done.

ANGÉLIQUE – Of that I am sure. But tell me more about our Abbot. Is he up to the job?

AGNÈS – He was the one whom I saw first, and in whom I found the most fire: there is no one more full of zest, and it is a pleasure to hear him discoursing. I was at recreation after dinner when someone came to tell me that he was asking for me. As I knew that Madame was not well, I asked the sister porter to direct him to the main parlour, and to bide his time there. I made him wait a good quarter of an hour, while I changed veil and wimple, so that I would appear before him looking at least decent, and try to live up to his hope of seeing a person who had been portrayed to him in such an advantageous light. When I arrived, I pretended to seem quite dumbstruck, replying with great seriousness to the civilities he uttered; but this did not take him aback; on the contrary, he took it as an opportunity to tell me quite boldly that he knew that beautiful women were permitted to speak casually, which would be unseemly in others, but that he had every cause to hope that, as he was presenting himself at the behest of my best lady friend, his visit could give me nothing but pleasure.

ANGÉLIQUE – He is considered to be a man of wit, and his long journeys, together with considerable experience, do seem to have added to his natural advantages whatever perfection he lacked.

AGNÈS – I do not know what you told him about me, but I feel that he was very forward for a first visit. He turned the conversation to the austerity of religious houses, and tried to persuade me, for countless reasons, not to follow the indiscreet zeal of the majority of them. He treated as ridiculous all those which were so stupid as to make use of such various forms of mortification. He made me laugh when he told me, quite straightforwardly, the story of something that had happened in Italy, with a nun of the order of Saint Benedict, and he described the cunning with which he had contrived to see her as often as he wished, eventually receiving from her the favours that were the due fruit of his assiduous courtship. He assured me that, faced with this habit, he had always thought that it was only among nuns that chastity had taken refuge and was still preserved, and that he had always been convinced that those secluded souls lived in a state of self-control as perfect as that of the angels; but he had now recognised that the complete opposite was true and that, since nothing perfect is only merely partly corrupted, and that a thing preserves in its corruption the same degree that it had before in its goodness, he had noticed that there was nothing more dissolute than all those reclusive nuns and bigots when they found an opportunity to amuse themselves. He showed me a certain glass instrument that he had been given by the aforementioned woman, and assured me that he had learned from her that there were over fifty similar things in their house and that all of the nuns, from the Abbess to the sister who had only just taken her vows, handled these implements more frequently than they did their rosaries.

ANGÉLIQUE – That is good. But you are not telling me anything about your own doings.

AGNÈS – What do you expect me to tell you? He is quite the playboy. On the second visit he paid me, I could not stop myself showing him some mercy. He opposed all my arguments with such a persuasive and cunning set of moral reasons that he rendered all my efforts useless. He showed me three letters from our Abbess which assured me that, whatever I might do, I would merely be following in her footsteps. She spent entire nights with him, and in her letters calls him nothing but the Abbé de Beaulieu. I pointed out to him that the grille was an insuperable obstacle, and that he would inevitably be obliged to content himself with superficial dallyings, since it was impossible to go any further. But he soon demonstrated that he knew more about these things than I did, and showed me two planks that could be lifted, one on his side and the other on mine, making it possible for one person to clamber through. He told me that it was on his advice that Madame had arranged matters thus, that she had named it the *Straits of Gibraltar*, and that she had told him, one day, that he should not venture to pass it without having armed himself with all the things necessary, especially if they were planning on stopping at the *Columns of Hercules*. So, after several attempts we both made, the Abbot passed the straits and arrived in harbour, where he was received, but this not without difficulty, and only after he had assured me that his entrance would not have any disagreeable consequences. I allowed him to stay there for as long as he needed to be happy; it was the seventh day of August, a day which Madame habitually employed in great ceremonies, but her illness had obliged her to postpone her normal observance of them for a month. He told me that she had created, during her second year as Abbess, an order of chivalry, which was composed only of priests, monks, abbots, religious and ecclesiastics; those who were admitted into it swore an oath to keep the order secret, and they were called the *Knights of the Grille*, or *of Saint Lawrence*. The necklet they were given on the day they were admitted to the order was composed of Madame's initials, interlaced in love knots, and at the bottom there hung a golden medallion representing the patron saint of the order, laid naked on a grill, amidst the flames, with these words: *Ardorem craticula fovet – The grill fans my flames.* He showed me the necklet he had received, and after giving me a few curious books as a present, we separated until our next interview.

ANGÉLIQUE – You have told me nothing new about the order established by Madame. M. the Bishop of *** is the first knight of the order, the Abbé de Beaumont is the second, the Abbé du Prat the third, and the Prior de Pompierre the fourth; those are the principals and the first in date. They are followed by Jesuits, Jacobins, Augustinians, Carmelites, Feuillants, Oratorians, and the Provincial of the Cordeliers. Indeed, at the final admission last year, there were twenty-two of them. But it is worth noting that there is a great deal of difference between them; they cannot all enjoy the same privileges. Some of them are called *blue ribbons*, and these are the ones who are all-powerful, holding the secrets of the order and arranging Madame's affairs, just as Madame conducts theirs. As far as the others are concerned, their power is restricted; there are limits which they cannot pass, and they have hardly any privileges than the aspirants – until, through their zeal, their prudence, and their discretion, they have made themselves worthy of being fully admitted to the great profession. Of all the monks, only Capuchins are excluded, since their beards – which disguise them so well – make them hateful to our Abbess, who says she cannot imagine that a person of the fair sex can feel any affection for these satyrs. But, by the way, tell me the latest about Father Vital de Charenton.

AGNÈS – I, like Madame, would never have thought that a Capuchin was capable of an amorous dalliance if that man had not persuaded me so by his behaviour. He came to see me three days after our Abbot; we went into the parlour of Saint Augustine's, and it was here that he treated me to more flowery words than I could have expected even from a professional courtier. Indeed, he spoke so boldly that I was ashamed to hear, from the lips of a man whose habit and beard preached nothing but penitence, words that were initially perfectly decent but eventually became more dissolute that those employed by the worst debauchee. I could not help but express my astonishment, and give him to understand that his transports were excessive: as a result, he moderated his tone somewhat. He paid me three visits during your retreat, and, at the final one, he obtained little from me, since the parlour in which we met did not have the comforts of that other parlour. I will merely say that he gave me considerable cause for mirth – for, having by his efforts dislodged one iron bar of the grille, and thinking that he had opened up a gap broad enough for him to pass through, he ventured into it in spite of my pleas, but could not force his way through, especially since, having with considerable difficulty passed his head and one of his shoulders through, his hood was caught on one of the jagged edges on the outside. However much he wriggled, he could not escape from this trap. I could not gaze at him in this posture without laughing. I promptly made him go back, and made him restore the grille to its prior state. He gave me three or four books which he had mentioned on his first visit, and withdrew, rather dissatisfied at his adventure.

ANGÉLIQUE – I am annoyed to hear of this accident. It will have put him off.

AGNÈS – Put him off? Good God! He is hardly the man to be put off! There is nobody more brazen than he: oh, he will be here before the week is out; he has promised me the *Collected*

Secret Loves of Robert d'Arbrissel. He started to tell me the story: but I think it is a whimsical fake, all made up.

ANGÉLIQUE – You are wrong; there is nothing more authentic, and several grave authors have written that he was accustomed to sleep with his nuns so as to test them, and simultaneously to discover, in his own person, how far the forces of virtue could go in their combat against the temptations of the flesh. He thought such deeds were highly meritorious, and this led Godefroy de Vendôme to treat this act of piety as silly and ridiculous in a letter he wrote to Saint Bernard, in which he calls this fervour a new type of martyrdom. This has so far prevented d'Arbrissel from being placed among the saints by the court of Rome. He is still, however, treated as a blessed.

AGNÈS – It has to be admitted that there are many abuses practised in our religion, and I am no longer surprised that so many people have separated from it in order to attach themselves to a literal reading of the Scriptures. The Feuillantine Father whom I saw during the retreat pointed out to me, very clearly, all the defects in the present system of government, as far as religion is concerned. He is a man who, for all his youth (he is only twenty-six) has already acquired all the knowledge that can make a person accomplished, whatever their character. He can speak about all things under the sun, but with a casual air – there is no whiff of pedantry about him.

ANGÉLIQUE – I can see that you have taken a liking to him. He is a fine figure of a fellow – a handsome lad. Personally, I only ever called him my *Great Whitecoat*. In which parlour did you see him?

AGNÈS – I saw him twice. The first time was in the parlour of Saint Joseph's, and the last time was in Madame's.

Angélique – Good, good! In other words, he passed *the straits*. He deserves it, and it is a pleasure to see him acting out his role.

Agnès – He gave me two small vials of essences that have a lovely smell. He was perfumed from head to feet, and showed such a lively crimson flush that I at first suspected he had been using the little pot; but I later realised that the opposite was true, and saw that his ruddy glow came merely from the ardour of his passion and the fact that his skin was nice and fresh. I greatly enjoyed talking to him and listening to his banter, and I found no difficulty in granting to him the passage from which I had so vigorously kept away our Abbot. I merely pointed out to him that there was some cause for anxiety lest the foolish things the two of us were doing led to a third. 'I understand,' he replied. So saying, he drew from his pocket a small book that he gave me: its title read *A Plain and Pleasant Path for Preventing a Problematic Plumpness*. He told me that I could learn from it what to do on such an occasion. He placed in my mouth a dollop of jam, which did not find taste too bad; I do not know if there was some secret virtue in it, but he immediately found himself in a state fit to reach the Columns of Hercules.

Angélique – So in other words, Great Whitecoat won your heart.

Agnès – Actually, he really shared it with the Abbot. I cannot say to whom I would give my preference. Just one thing shocked me about the Feuillant: having seen around his neck a reliquary of gilded vermilion that he wore over his heart, I felt curious, and opened it; but I was greatly surprised to find nothing there but hair from the head and the body, all in different colours, divided into very neatly decorated compartments. He confessed that these were the favours of all his mistresses, and begged me to favour his devotions too, saying that the loveliest place would serve best, from which to take what I kindly granted him. What do you expect? I satisfied him. I was forgetting to tell you that there was this inscription in golden letters, in the middle of a crystal covering this fine piece of merchandise: *Reliques of Saint Barbe*. On the lid of the reliquary you could see the engraving of a Cupid on a throne, and our man lying prostrate at his feet, with these words (I remember them clearly, even though they are in Latin): AVE LEX, JUS, AMOR. I rebuked him for this irreverence, and said it was quite impious; but he merely laughed and replied that he could not withhold his worship from those women, who deserved every kind of adoration; if I were able to decipher seven other letters on the other side, I would have even more cause for surprise. And indeed, having looked, I saw the seven following letters: A.C.D.E.D.L.G. He always refused to explain them to me, however much I begged him. I pretended to be annoyed: but he soon realised that I was not really angry with him: that is why he embraced me again, and we took our leave of each other.

ANGÉLIQUE – I am delighted, my dear child, that everything passed off just as I wished; this is just one example of what I wish to do for you, and I will arrange for you to make the acquaintance of a Jesuit to whom, no doubt, you will award the prize, admitting that he has beaten all the others. But he is jealous to a fault of his little habits: that is the sole failing you will find in him. Apart from that, he is a handsome fellow, gallant, a fine talker, well acquainted with everything that may come to a person's knowledge.

AGNÈS – That is a big enough failing to stop me getting on with him.

ANGÉLIQUE – Oh? Why is that? You will find it very difficult to find a man who is capable of true love while not being jealous. I remember that I knew a Benedictine who thought that all the nuns in the order of Saint Benedict could not so much as see a man from a different order without committing an unjust thought: they were stealing from him and his colleagues all the favours that they granted to the Capuchins. And this is how he argued: 'No one can doubt that men of religion are subject to the same passions and impulses as those who live in the world. It is with this in mind,' he said, 'that the founders of religious orders, who were extremely enlightened, did not build cloisters for those of their own sex unless they at the same time built cloisters for girls, so that, without resorting to strangers, both groups could from time to time relieve themselves from the rigours of their vows. To begin with, this was practised in accordance with the intentions of those who had set up these institutions, which meant that there was no scandal; but these days, such places are filled with the stench of general corruption. It is easy to see a Bernardine monk with a Jacobin nun, a Cordelier monk with a Benedictine nun – and from this horrible confusion, only monsters can be born.'

AGNÈS – That was rather an amusing idea.

ANGÉLIQUE – 'Alas!' he exclaimed, 'what would all those founding saints say at the sight of so many adulteries, if they were to come back to earth? How many thunderbolts they would hurl, how many anathemas they would fulminate against their own children! Would not Saint Francis send the Capuchin monks back to the Capuchin nuns, the he-Cordeliers to the she-Cordeliers? Would not Saint Dominic, Saint Bernard and all the others send all those who had strayed back to the original road of their rules and constitutions? The Jacobin monks to the Jacobin nuns, I mean, and the he-Fueillants to the she-Fueillants?'

'But what would happen to the Jesuits and the Carthusians?' I asked. 'After all, neither Saint Ignatius nor Saint Bruno drew up any rules for the fair sex.'

'Oh,' he replied, 'but that Spaniard *did* make excellent provisions on that score! He did so on purpose, so that they would have a reason for going everywhere with impunity. And in addition, following his imagination, which was somewhat inclined to pederasty, he placed them in positions where they can find with young people moments of satisfaction that they prefer to all the amusements of others.

'As for the Carthusians,' he continued, 'since they are strictly ordered to live in seclusion, they seek in themselves the pleasure that they cannot go out to find from others, and by a harsh and violent war they overcome the most intense temptations of the flesh. They reiterate the combat for as long as their enemy resists them; they employ all their vigour on it, and call that sort of expedition *the war of five against one*.' Well now: did not the disciple of Saint Bernard speak words of wisdom?

AGNÈS – Assuredly, I would be delighted to hear more.

ANGÉLIQUE – There is nothing more certain than that, if this were indeed the practice and if, even in debauch, some rule were followed, everything would be better. A year ago, a certain young nun would not have been so unhappy as she has been ever since if she had done with the provincial of her order what she did with that of another. You may have heard of Sister Cécile and Father Raymond?

AGNÈS – No; tell me what you know about them.

ANGÉLIQUE – Sister Cécile is a nun of the order of Saint Augustine, and Father Raymond was at that time the provincial of the Jacobins. I will not tell you how he insinuated his way into the mind of that innocent girl, who had been inaccessible to all other men up until then; but I will tell you this much – he won her over to such an extent that never has there been a closer friendship, and they could not go for a moment without seeing each other or receiving news of one another. Their intimacy was noticed in the community, and the Augustinian provincial who was in charge of this house, having learnt what was happening, was in a state of despair: never had he managed to obtain any favours from her, even though he had resorted to every means of corrupting her. She was the most beautiful nun in the convent. So, being profoundly shocked and hurt, he wrote to the Mother Superior and ordered her to keep an eye on Cécile's behaviour. It was easy for this guardian Mother rapidly to discover some evidence of foolish behaviour, since nothing was being done to hide it; it was merely a matter of amorous banter – but this was still enough to give a jealous man in a position of power an excuse to mistreat a poor nun. Yet he did not decide to do so, intending instead to use this opportunity to gain from her what he had not been able to obtain before. He wrote to her in person, so that nothing would come to public notice, and forbade her to use the grille until he arrived. He lived twenty leagues away.

Agnès – But was it possible to produce any evidence to prove against her that she had done anything unusual?

Angélique – Oh, how easy it is to find such proofs, even if there are none, when one is intent on destroying a person! But the whole problem arose merely because she had been ill advised. So when the provincial arrived, he told her that it was on the basis of information that he had received about her misbehaviour that he had brought himself hither; that it

48

was a shameful thing for a young nun like her to abandon herself to actions that could not even be named, being so vile; and that he was highly displeased to see himself obliged to make an exemplary punishment of her. Cécile, who was guilty before men of nothing more than a little fond banter, of looking and touching, said that it was true that she had very often seen the Father Raymond just mentioned, but that she had done nothing with him that might merit any real reprobation; she had said her farewells to him as soon as she had been ordered to do so, and had thereby demonstrated that there was nothing particularly close in their relationship. In order to achieve his ends, the provincial changed tack and spoke to her more gently, pointing out that, if any mortification were to be imposed on her, she herself would be to blame; she could remedy the wrong she had done, and easily avoid the rigorous correction that would inevitably be imposed upon her, if she availed herself of the advantages that she possessed. At the same time he took her by the hand, squeezing it amorously and gazing at her with a smile that was meant to indicate to her the heartfelt sentiments that her, her judge, felt for her.

AGNÈS – Did she not use her allure to save herself from the danger that threatened?

ANGÉLIQUE – No; she adopted a line of conduct that was entirely the opposite of that she should have followed: she took it into her head that her provincial was talking to her like this merely to test her, and that his sole intent was to judge, from her weakness, of what she might have done with the other man. On the basis of this false reasoning, she merely replied to the provincial, burning as he was with love for her, in frigid tones and words which were worse than casual, and which changed the heart of that ardent suitor and transformed him from a tender lover into an implacable judge. So he proceeded, in all due form, to put Cécile on trial; he heard the statements that jealousy and flattery placed in the mouths of several of her companions, and finally sentenced the poor girl to be whipped until blood was drawn, to fast for ten Fridays on bread and water, and to be excluded from the parlour for six months. So one can say that she was punished for having been too well-behaved, and for not having allowed herself to be corrupted by the brutality of her superior.

Agnès – Oh God! I find that *so* touching! I regard that poor nun as an innocent victim, sacrificed to the rage of a madman, and cannot see any difference between her and the eleven thousand virgins.

Angélique – You are right, for it is said they were slaughtered for refusing to satisfy a man's passion, and this girl was merely insulted for the same reason. Since there is no animal in the world more lustful than a monk, there is likewise none more malign and more vindictive when his ardour is scorned. I have read on this subject the story of a wicked Capuchin, in a book whose title was *The Goat On Heat*. But, incidentally, tell me… what were the books that you were given during my retreat?

Agnès – Gladly; some of them were quite amusing. Here is the list:

> *Fecund Chastity*, a curious short novel.
> *The Jesuits' Master Key*, a gallant play.
> *The Prison Enlightened*, or *The Opening of the Little Shutter*, fully illustrated.
> *The Day Labourer of the Feuillantine Nuns.*
> *The Valiant Achievements of the Knights of Saint Lawrence.*

Rules and Statutes of the Abbey of Bangit-in-Hard.
Collection of Remedies against Perilous Plumpness,
composed for the commodity of the religious ladies
of Saint-Georges.
The Extreme Unction of Expiring Virginity.
The Apostolic Quack composed by the four beggars,
ex praecepto Sanctissimi.
The Monks' Arse-Cutter.
The Abbots' Pastime.
The War of the Carthusians.
The Fruits of the Unitive Life.

Unless I am mistaken, I do not think I have forgotten
any on this list. I have already read five or six of them, with
considerable enjoyment.

ANGÉLIQUE – Indeed – they have given you an entire library.
If the inside is anything like the outside, as I do not doubt it
is, these books must be extremely entertaining. You will find
in them everything you need to complete your education
and make yourself the kind of woman you need to be,
expert in every kind of knowledge under the sun: for there
are people who, in the midst of great enlightenment, still
have their doubts, which sometimes cause them considerable pain, and which often have dangerous consequences.
On this very subject I am going to tell you a story that happened in the Abbey of Chelles.

AGNÈS – You must be a mistress of intrigue to find out all the
most secret things that happen in the religious houses.

ANGÉLIQUE – Well, the Abbess of this house, being by nature
very hot-blooded, was accustomed to taking a bath during
the midsummer weeks. The bath was run in accordance with
the instructions of her doctor who, so that it would be found
more pleasant, prescribed a rule and a particular method to

be observed, without which the bath would be useless. On the evening of the day before the Abbess was to take the bath, it had to be made completely ready and the water allowed to rest all night until the following day, when it was possible, at certain times, to get into it. There was no lack of odours and essences; they were profusely scattered into the water, and everything which could pander to Madame's sensuality was included in the mixture.

AGNÈS – It is doctors who, by a wrongheaded sense of complaisance, thus indulge peoples' weaknesses.

ANGÉLIQUE – Be that as it may, a young nun of the house named Sister Scolastique, aged eighteen, on seeing all these great preparations for Madame and noticing that the bath was all ready the evening before, decided – in order to find relief from the discomforts of the season as well as from her inner heat, which was quite intense – to take advantage of the occasion and to try out this salutary *lavabo*[2] for herself every evening. Indeed, for a whole week she did not miss a single evening, and found that this gave a certain lustre to her plump body, and that she felt better rested as a result. She would emerge from her room at around nine o'clock and, almost naked, in her chemise, betake herself to the place where everything stood ready: she soon slipped out of her skirt and her chemise and thus, completely naked, sat herself down in the tub, where she washed and rubbed herself all over, and then climbed out as pure and clean as Eve in the earthly paradise during her state of innocence.

AGNÈS – Did nobody see her?

ANGÉLIQUE – I am just coming to that. One evening, as Scolastique was refreshing her body in her usual way, an old nun who had not yet gone to sleep, having heard someone walking down the corridor at a time when, as custom dictated, all the nuns were supposed to have withdrawn for the night, came out of her room and, after having looked around in vain for the person she had heard, went into the place where the bath was, and immediately noticed, in the silver moonlight, a completely naked nun wiping herself with a towel before putting her chemise back on. The old dear, thinking that it must be the Abbess, promptly withdrew, apologising for having blundered in. Scolastique did not say a thing, but realised that the reverend mother had made a mistake, and had taken her for another woman. She went off, having given the other nun time to withdraw, and decided never to return, in case she was discovered.

AGNÈS – And did everything end there?

ANGÉLIQUE – No. If only it had, poor Scolastique's buttocks would have felt pretty relieved.

AGNÈS – What? Did that lovely child have to face any hassle?

ANGÉLIQUE – The venerable mother I mentioned, having reflected in the morning on what she had seen the evening before, thought it would be a good idea to go and see Madame, and make an individual apology for her clumsy entrance, which Madame might have attributed to unhealthy curiosity: and this she did, unfortunately. The Abbess was most surprised, and deduced that she herself had been bathing in the dirty water left over by some sick woman in her community. She spoke of it the next day in her chapter, and commanded the woman who had sat in the bath to declare it, in virtue of *holy obedience*; but not one in the company spoke. Scolastique was not the most truthful of girls, and had her wits about her; thus she stayed silent. This general silence threw the Abbess into despair. She shouted, she fulminated, she threatened everyone – but all in vain. Finally, on the advice of a monk, she decided on a most pleasant stratagem. She assembled all her nuns and admonished them, saying that there was one of them who was excommunicate, and in a state of damnation, for not having revealed what she had been commanded to say *in virtue of holy obedience*; a wise and holy man had given her a sure and infallible means of discovering the guilty woman, but she would give the culprit a chance to speak and thereby avoid the harsh penances that she would incur by her blatant disobedience.

AGNÈS – Oh God! What a terrible situation! I fear for poor Scolastique; the advice of monks is always pernicious.

ANGÉLIQUE – When Madame saw that this last threat had been without effect, she followed the advice she had been given. She had a table in a room covered with a pall; in the middle, she had a chalice from the sacristy placed. When things had been arranged as she ordered, she commanded all her girls to enter one after the other and to touch with their hands the foot of the sacred vessel (these were her words) displayed on the table; by this means, she would discover who exactly had kept herself concealed until now, since, as soon as she had placed her fingers on that sacred cup, the table would crash to the ground and, by a secret virtue from on high, reveal which woman was the guilty party. This all happened at nine o'clock in the evening, and in darkness. So all the nuns entered this room and touched the foot of the chalice. Scolastique was the only one who did not dare to do so, for fear of being discovered, and merely touched the mat on which it stood. After which, she withdrew with the others into a second room that was also unlit, from where the Abbess summoned them to her one by one once the whole ceremony had been performed. Now, you need to know that she had blackened the foot of the chalice with oil

54

and soot, so that it was impossible to touch it without carrying away the marks from it. So, having lit a candle in the room where she was, the Abbess examined the hands of all the nuns and realised that they had all touched the cup, except for Scolastique, who had no smudges on her fingers, unlike the others in the community. This led her to conclude that it was she who had committed the crime. The poor innocent, seeing herself deceived by a false artifice, resorted to tears and excuses; she got off with a couple of floggings, which were administered in front of the whole company. Well, it was merely this outer show of religious ritual, here put to impious use, that had made her afraid, and if she had reflected just a little on the impossibility of being found out by such a ridiculous artifice, she would never have been discovered.

AGNÈS – That is true; but the Abbess should have forgiven her beauty and her youth.

ANGÉLIQUE – She could have done so, but she did not, and I have even heard that the first lashing she ordered to be inflicted on her lasted for nearly a quarter of an hour. So just imagine the state in which the lovely child's buttocks must have been!

AGNÈS – They were probably more or less like mine, when I showed them to you. If I could have my wish, I would condemn to permanent imprisonment in the hulks the Abbess's cursed councillor, and if that had happened to me, I would lay so many ambushes for that monk, with the help of a few girl friends from the outside world, that I would make him repent of his stratagem.

ANGÉLIQUE – Do you believe that, if he had thought that Scolastique were to be chastised like that, he would have given a hand to detecting her misdeed? No: he imagined, as did the Abbess, that it was some old or infirm woman who had been caught in the act; and this is what made Madame feel so sick at heart – the thought that she had, as she imagined, washed in the filth of such persons.

AGNÈS – For my part, I think she was relieved when she realised that it was Scolastique who had sat in her bath, since a young girl who is clean and attractive, as you have described her to me, is never an object of disgust. The penance she was given makes me think of that given to Virginie and to the children of the Jesuit's square bonnet.

ANGÉLIQUE – I must show you a couple of those children that I have here in my little box: there is one from Father de Raucourt, and the other is from Virginie. Here you are, read this one.

AGNÈS – This almost looks like a girl's handwriting – it appears carelessly written:

Oh God! My dear child, how this exchange of letters is starting to weary me! It is merely fanning my flames, instead of giving them any relief; it tells me that Virginie loves me, but it immediately makes it clear that it is impossible to enjoy her. Ah, how this mixture of sweetness and bitterness causes strange movements in a heart fashioned like mine! I had indeed heard that love sometimes gave wit to those lacking in it, but in myself I sense the opposite effect, and I can truly say that it takes away from me what it gives to others. Several people notice this change, but they do not know the reason for it. Yesterday, I preached to the nuns of the Visitation: never had I been more animated. I was supposed, in conformity with my subject, to speak to the company on mortification and penitence, and in my whole discourse I spoke of nothing but affections, of tenderness, of outbursts of passion and of transports. It is you, Virginie, who are the cause of all this disorder. So, take pity on my confusion of mind, and contrive to find a quick means of bringing me back to my senses. Farewell.

ANGÉLIQUE – Well, Agnès, what do you have to say about this hastily conceived child?

AGNÈS – I find it worthy of its father, and capable – all bare as it is of dress and adornment – not merely of keeping a heart that it possesses faithful to it, but even of exciting new movements within it.

ANGÉLIQUE – You are right; for in love, the most negligent style is always the most persuasive, and often all the eloquence of an orator could not arouse in a soul those sweet transports that are simply the effects of an inconspicuous and yet expressive term. This is a truth to which I can bear witness, since I have experienced it several times within myself. But let us see whether Virginie expresses herself as well as her lover.

AGNÈS – Give me the letter, I would like to read it.

ANGÉLIQUE – Here you are; it is a note rather than a letter, since the whole thing consists of just five or six lines.

AGNÈS – Its handwriting is very similar to mine:

Ah, how artful you are in your words and how well you know how to disturb what little peace of mind an innocent woman who loves you still retains! Can you reasonably ask me whether I am thinking of you? Alas, my dear! Look into your own heart, and believe me when I tell you that we cannot both be animated by one and the same passion, unless we feel the same wounds. Farewell; endeavour to break our chains: love makes me capable of anything. Ah, how weak it makes me feel! Farewell.

ANGÉLIQUE – Do you not find this note much more tender than the letter?

AGNÈS – Assuredly; it seems to be all heart, and two or three sentences express the disposition of the soul of a woman in love just as well as would two pages of a novel. But I do not think it is a reply to the letter that we read from Father de Raucourt.

ANGÉLIQUE – No, it is not one; it is the reply to another letter that was not sent to me.

AGNÈS – I am touched by the misfortune of these two lovers; I feel an extreme compassion for the travails of Virginie; for she is probably passing her time at present in a great deal of sorrow, and leading a very wearisome life.

ANGÉLIQUE – If she had not kept the letters and notes that were addressed to her, she would not be so unhappy; for her intention to leave the convent would never have come to light.

AGNÈS – So that is probably what she means when she says, in her note: *Endeavour to break our chains.* I would not have given her words their real meaning. Ah! How unhappy she would have been, poor girl, if she had committed this wicked deed! Alas! Of what is love not capable, when it finds itself opposed?

ANGÉLIQUE – As soon as the rector of the Jesuits had learned what was happening, from the letter he found in the bonnet, he informed the Mother Superior, who immediately went with her assistant to search Virginie's room, where she found, in her little box, countless notes and other trifles that revealed to her the truth of what she could never had believed had she not herself seen it. Since she loved Virginie dearly, she allowed to be revealed only what could not be concealed, and she moderated the chastisement prescribed by the regulations.

AGNÈS – The Jesuit was more fortunate – he was obliged merely to change province.

ANGÉLIQUE – Oh, but the business did not pass itself off as quietly as you imagine! He is at present exiled from the company. You know, since in a society everything turns on esteem and reputation, and is established on them alone, it is impossible for a man of honour to remain in that society once he has lost, through some accident, in the minds of his colleagues, those two things which so agreeably flatter men's ambitions. So Father de Raucourt, seeing that he had fallen, in the misfortune you know of, from that height of glory which he had obtained by his merits, and in which he had always maintained himself by his prudence, disdained the indulgence that his superiors were offering him, and decided thereupon to abandon them: he did so a short while ago, and has retired to England.

AGNÈS – But a man whose only possessions are knowledge and whose only inheritance is philosophy – whatever can he do in a foreign land?

ANGÉLIQUE – What can he do? He can use his mind to make himself more useful to the republic (if it wishes to employ him) than all the artisans that comprise it. He can by his writings give vigour to the laws that are most opposed to the people's mere inclinations. He can convey a nation's glory to the most distant places. Finally, there are few professions that he cannot worthily fill, or from which the State cannot draw much fruit. I have reason on my side, and evidence too: I have learned from a Dominican that a malcontent of their order was at the court of that kingdom to which de Raucourt has retired, and that he was there cutting a very fine figure as a resident or envoy of a certain German prince.

AGNÈS – Doubtless he would have taken Virginie to that country, if they had put their plans into action. Alas! How few men and women would lead the monastic life of seclusion, if all those entering the cloister were given time to reflect on the advantages of an honest liberty and the disagreeable consequences of a fateful commitment!

ANGÉLIQUE – What makes you say that? Can we not, within the enclosure of our walls, enjoy pleasures as perfect as those who live outside? The obstacles raised against them serve merely to give them greater relish when, after having skilfully overcome those obstacles, we possess what we desired. It would be wicked and ungrateful to censure the diversions of monks and monkesses, for I would say to such people: Is it not true that self-control is a gift of God, a present with which he gratifies whomever it pleases him, and which he does not grant to those whom he does not wish to honour with it? Supposing that is so, he will not expect an account of this present from any except those to whom he has given it.

AGNÈS – I can easily understand the force of that reason; but it might be said that the vows by which we solemnly commit ourselves make us responsible before him.

ANGÉLIQUE – Ah! And can you not see that those vows, which you make at the hands of men, are so much hot air? Can you reasonably oblige him to give what you do not have and cannot have if such is not the will of him whom you are asking to grant it? So judge of the nature of our promises, and ask whether, strictly speaking, we are held, before God, to keep our promises, since they contain within themselves a moral impossibility. You cannot say anything to overturn this argument.

AGNÈS – That is true; and that is what must quieten our minds.

ANGÉLIQUE – For my part, I can tell you that nothing causes me any sorrow. I spend my time in an evenness of temper that renders me insensible to the pains that harass others. I see everything, I hear everything; but few things are able to move me, and if my repose had not been disturbed by a bodily indisposition, there would be nobody able to live with greater tranquillity than myself.

AGNÈS – But, given this behaviour – so different from that in other cloisters – what do you think of the disposition of their souls? And do not those actions that are followed, as they preach, by so many merits, tempt you by the hope they offer? It might be argued against us that libertinage can often provide us with the causes of our destruction. For what is more holy than meditating on heavenly things, an activity in which they employ themselves? What is more praiseworthy than that lofty piety that they practise; and can the fasts and austerities with which they mortify themselves be considered so many fruitless works?

ANGÉLIQUE – Ah, my child, how feeble are those objections! You need to know that there is a great difference between licence and liberty: in my actions, I often stand on the slope of the latter, but I never allow myself to fall into the debauchery of the former. If I do not place any limits on my joy and my pleasures, that is because they are innocent, and never wound by excess the things which I must hold in veneration. But you really want me to tell you what I think about those melancholy madmen whose manners bewitch you. Do you know that what you call 'the contemplation of divine things' is at bottom merely a soft and cowardly sloth, incapable of any action; that the impulses of that heroic piety that so dazzles you proceed merely from the disorder of a corrupted reason, and that if you seek the general cause that makes them tear themselves to pieces like desperate men, you will find it in the vapours of a black humour, or in the weakness of their brains?

AGNÈS – I take such pleasure in hearing your arguments that I deliberately suggest as a difficulty something that did not in fact allow the shadow of a doubt… but I can hear the bell calling us.

ANGÉLIQUE – It is time to go to the refectory. After dinner, we will be able to continue our conversation.

THIRD CONVERSATION
SISTER AGNÈS, SISTER ANGÉLIQUE

AGNÈS – Ah, how delightful the day is! It awakens all my spirits. Let us both withdraw down this pathway, and leave the others to themselves.

ANGÉLIQUE – We could not have found a spot better suited to strolling in the whole garden, since the trees surrounding it will afford us as much shade as we need not to be exposed to the heat of the sun.

AGNÈS – That is true; but it is to be feared that Madame may come here for rest and relaxation, since this is where she most often chooses to take the air after a meal.

ANGÉLIQUE – Do not worry that she will chase us away: she is not feeling too well just now; and if you knew the reason for her indisposition, you would not be able to stop laughing.

AGNÈS – But she was perfectly well yesterday.

ANGÉLIQUE – Indeed. The malady befell her only in the night, and you must have been deeply asleep not to have been aware of how, by her cries, she alarmed the whole dormitory. I had decided to amuse myself by telling you came I went to fetch you this morning, but our conversation gradually drew me away from the topic.

AGNÈS – It is true that I learn the latest news only when it is already public knowledge.

ANGÉLIQUE – As you know, one of Madame's principal pleasures lies in feeding all sorts of animals. She does not content herself with countless birds from every country – she has even made pets of animals such as tortoises and fish. Since she makes no attempt to conceal this eccentricity, and all her friends know that she calls this occupation the delight of her solitude, they all endeavour to contribute to her amusement, by making a present to her, sometimes of one animal and sometimes of another. When the Abbé de Saint-Valéry learned that she had even tamed (for so he had been told) some carp and pike, he sent her, four days ago, two live scoter ducks and two big sea crayfish, all alive. After cutting the wings off those half-ducks, she had them thrown into the fish tank, and decided to devote herself entirely to raising the crayfish. With this in mind, she had a little wooden bowl brought into her room, and filled it with water, and placed the lobsters (this is another name for these animals) in it. I would find it quite difficult to detail all the trouble she took to preserve them; she would even toss them sweets and pistachios. Eventually, she refused to feed them with anything except the most delicate meats.

AGNÈS – Such pastimes as these are innocent, and excusable when one is young.

ANGÉLIQUE – Yesterday evening, by some misfortune, Sister Olinde, who had been instructed to change the water in the bowl every day to refresh the fish, completely forgot; this is what caused all the hubbub. Well, since last night was very hot, one of those lobsters, who found itself incommoded by the great heat, climbed out of the bowl, and dragged itself round the room for quite a while, until, deciding that it had found some relief, again sought the water it had quitted, as this was after all its most natural element. But since it had been much easier for the creature to climb out than to climb back in, it was obliged to resort to the water in Madame's chamber pot, where, without examining whether it contained fresh or salt water, it took refuge. Some time later, our Abbess needed to piss; half asleep and not even bothering to climb out of bed, she picked up her urinary receptacle; but alas! She almost died of shock! This crayfish, who felt itself being sprinkled by water that seemed a little too warm, lunged at the place from which the liquid appeared to be descending, and pinched it so tight with one of its claws that it left marks there for over three days.

Agnès – Ha! Ha! Ha! What a tale! That is just *so* hilarious!

Angélique – She straightaway uttered a cry that awoke all her neighbours; she flung the chamber pot to the ground and, jumping to her feet, called everyone to her aid. However, this animal, which had never found such a delicate and tasty morsel, would just not let go. The Mother Assistant and Sister Cornélie were the quickest to leap out of their beds; they had to stifle their laughter at the sight of such a spectacle, but they contained their mirth as well as they could, and were obliged to cut off the claw of this sacrilegious beast, which had hitherto refused to let go of its prey. The Mother Assistant withdrew, and Sister Cornelia, who is Madame's confidante, spent the rest of the night with her, to console her. That is the reason why our Abbess is not feeling well, and it will obviously prevent her from coming along and interrupting our conversations.

Agnès – Ah! I would never show my face, if such an accident had happened to me, and had come to the knowledge of other people.

Angélique – Indeed, there is plenty for her to be ashamed about! She did not reveal anything that she has not often revealed to others, and the knights of the order have on many occasions placed their hands just where the crayfish placed its claw.

Agnès – Which of these is her best friend?

Angélique – I do not know – but I do know that a Jesuit visits her frequently, and has shared intimacies with her, which demonstrate that he is one of the *blue ribbons*. I spotted her one day with him engaged in highly animated conversation, and, on one other occasion when she was coming away from seeing the same person, I found in the parlour that she had just left a thin towel, with damp stains of a somewhat viscous liquid on it: she had dropped it near the window. I did not mention this encounter; I merely noticed that losing this towel left her feeling rather anxious.

AGNÈS – So what does she have to fear? The Bishop on whom she solely depends is at her discretion, and when he visited this convent, he issued no orders other than those that *she* had previously prescribed to *him*.

ANGÉLIQUE – Too right. She is mistress of everything: and spiritual directors and confessors are appointed and changed only at her behest.

AGNÈS – Ah! I only wish, with all my heart, that she disliked the ordinary confessor we have at present as much as I do! What is your opinion?

ANGÉLIQUE – It is true that he is very austere, and capable of making a great deal of trouble for women who cannot behave themselves; but as for the rest of us, it must be a matter of complete indifference whether it is he, or someone less rigorous, who hears our confessions.

AGNÈS – For my part, I cannot tell him of the least peccadillo without him flying into a rage. If I confess a particular thought, he imposes horrible mortifications and penances on me, and makes me fast for two whole days for the least carnal impulse that I confess; and most of the time I do not know what to tell him, for fear of saying something that will shock him. I cannot imagine how you manage – you keep him listening for such a long time.

ANGÉLIQUE – Come now, do you think I am so stupid as to declare to him my heart's secrets? Far from it: since I know that he is so very strict, I tell him only things over which he has no authority. The only conclusion he can draw from my disclosures is that I am girl who spends her time in prayer and contemplation, who is unacquainted with the impulses of corrupt nature... and so he does not dare even ask me about such things. The harshest penance I have had is five *paternosters* and the *Litanies*.

AGNÈS – But what on earth do you tell him, then? Merely for breaking silence, or for making fun of someone in the community (which are trivial offences) he sermonises me for quarter of an hour.

ANGÉLIQUE – All those misdemeanours are designated, individually and with all the circumstantial details, as minor – but they sometimes become more considerable, and that is what makes you subject to his rebukes. But look, this is how I go about it: listen to my latest confession. Having most humbly asked for his blessing, with my eyes lowered, my hands clasped, and my body half bent forwards, I start like this:

My Father, I am the greatest sinner in the world, and the most feeble of creatures: I fall almost always into the same sins.

I accuse myself of having disturbed the tranquillity of my soul by universal divagations that have turned everything within me upside down;

of not having had enough concentration of mind and having wasted too much energy on outward business;

of having stayed too long at the level of mere intellectual understanding, spending most of my time for prayer on that level instead of attending to my will, which has remained dry and sterile as a result;

of having, on another occasion, allowed myself to be first bound by my affections, and subsequently exposed to troublesome distractions and to a slothfulness of spirit that is quite contrary to the methodical perfection of the contemplatives;

of having clutched too tightly within myself at everything that came from myself, instead of freeing my heart from all created things, by a noble act of annihilation of my self-love, of my interests, desires and wishes, and of my whole self;

of having made an offering of my heart, without having previously quietened it and cleansed it of the uproar of over-restless passions and uncontrolled affections;

of having allowed myself to be too much swept away by the inclinations of the old Adam and the tendencies of unregenerate Nature, instead of separating myself from everything in order to gain everything;

of not having taken due care to renew myself by reviewing myself, within myself, and to repair within myself what of myself was fallen, etc.

Well! Agnès, you can judge of the whole cloth from this sample. This is not a third of my confession, but the rest does not make me any more criminal than this beginning.

AGNÈS – It is true that I would be really flummoxed if I had to impose penances on sins that had been confessed with such wit. However, that is the only way of putting off the track the curiosity of the younger spiritual directors, and avoiding the rebukes of the older ones.

ANGÉLIQUE – The latter are usually the most intractable; since I have been in the convent, I have rarely seen any of the younger ones who did not tend to be rather indulgent.

AGNÈS – True – they are not all equally rigorous: witness the director who so pushed the claims of piety into the souls of certain of our sisters that they found themselves in a rather uncomfortable situation nine months later.

ANGÉLIQUE – Oh God! How much cunning they needed to hide that one, and to prevent anyone outside learning of it! The Bishop himself found out only when any further proof was lacking. This reminds me of an Italian Jesuit who, one day when he was hearing the confession of a young French gentleman who had learned the language of the country, unthinkingly uttered an exclamation that gave away his particular weakness. The penitent accused himself of having spent the night with a girl from one of the foremost families in Rome, and of having enjoyed her as he desired. The good Father, gazing attentively at the man talking to him (a handsome lad with a fine physique) quite forgot his position and, imagining that he was taking part in some free-and-easy chatter (and feeling quite aroused to boot), asked the young man if this girl was beautiful, how old she might be, and how much he had actually done with her. The French man replied that he had found her to be of consummate beauty, she was only eighteen, and he had kissed her three times. '*Ah! Qual gusto! Signor!*' he then exclaimed quite fervently, meaning 'Ah! Such pleasure!'

AGNÈS – Rather a comic little outburst – and most likely to excite the penitent's heart to repentance for his sin.

ANGÉLIQUE – What do you expect? They are men like others. And I have heard from one of my friends who was employed on such tasks that often a confessor would expose himself less to the temptations of lust if he went to a brothel than he would by listening to the words spoken into his ear by women of religion.

AGNÈS – For my part, I think I would find the occupation of confessor rather entertaining, so long as I were allowed to choose my penitents: I would enjoy listening to them, and my imagination would be deeply stirred by the stories they told me of their foolish misdeeds. And this would give me great satisfaction.

ANGÉLIQUE – Alas! My child! You do not know what you are asking. If one woman of religion gives a little pleasure to a confessor by the innocent narrative of her little failings, there are a thousand who weary them with their scruples. Confessors would find it easier to pull such nuns out of a chasm than to free from their doubts. Sister Dosithée, all by herself, spent over three years keeping the general spiritual of the house busy with her questions. However much he pointed out to her that the over-curious self-examination with which she harassed her conscience – for she never felt that she had taken enough care in the matter – was not only useless, but even wrong, and contrary to perfection. He could not prevail against her, and was obliged to abandon her to herself, and to leave her in a state of error.

AGNÈS – However, these days she is quite sensible, and I remember that once, when we were obliged to sleep in the same bed while our dormitory was being raised, she spoke to me in terms which were not only far removed from any moral scruple, but which I even found, in those days, a little too licentious, not to mention the countless amorous whims to which she aroused me by telling me a hundred of the most lubricious and lascivious tales in the world.

ANGÉLIQUE – You obviously do not how she emerged from the darkness in which superstition had so deeply immersed her. Her confessor played no part in her deliverance. One could say that it was her piety itself which produced this change,

and which transformed her from being an extremely punctilious girl into a perfectly sensible nun. I would like to tell
you what I learned from her own account.

AGNÈS – I cannot imagine such a thing. Saying that piety can
rid a person of her scruples is the same as saying that one
blind man can pull another blind man away from a precipice.

ANGÉLIQUE – Just listen to me, and you will realise that I am
telling you the plain truth and nothing but. Sister Dosithée,
as one can see from her eyes, was born with the most tender
and most amorous constitution in the world. The poor girl,
on entering the religious life, fell into the hands of an elderly
spiritual director, as ignorant as you can imagine, and all the
more a hater of nature because his age made him incapable
of enjoying all the pleasures that nature offered. So, recog-
nising that it was the pleasures of the flesh for which his
penitent had a penchant, and that the sins of which she
accused herself every day were a sure and certain proof
thereof, he decided that it was his duty to reform that nature
– which in his view was corrupt – and that he was qualified
to set himself up as a second redeemer. In order to achieve
his aims, he cast into her soul the seeds of every kind of
scruple, every doubt and pricking of conscience, that he
could imagine. He was all the more successful in this
endeavour in that he found her already disposed to listen to
him, and the candid confessions that he had often heard
from this innocent girl had acquainted him with her extreme sensitivity on the matter of her salvation.

So he depicted to her the path to heaven in such harsh
colours that they would have been capable of making a less
zealous and less fervent person than she was turn away from
it with horror. He spoke of nothing but the destruction of
the body, opposed as it was to the bliss of the spirit; and the

horrible penances which he forced on her were, according to him, absolutely necessary means for her to reach the heavenly Jerusalem.

Dosithée, unable to defend herself from these arguments, allowed herself blindly to be led by the indiscreet piety with which she became infatuated; the simple practice of God's commands now seemed to her to be of little worth in his eyes; works of supererogation were necessary too; and indeed, with all this train of virtues, she was still in a state of continuous fear of the torments of the next world with which she was so often threatened. Since it is impossible, here below, to destroy what is called 'concupiscence' in us, she was never at peace with herself; it was a ceaseless war that she imprudently waged with her poor body, and the terrible fight that she put up against it was rarely followed by any truce.

AGNÈS – Alas! How she was to be pitied, and how much compassion she would have inspired in me if I had seen her stuck in this foolish endeavour!

ANGÉLIQUE – Since her amorous nature was, in her eyes, the source of her greatest failings, she neglected no means of quenching her most innocent flames; fasts and hair-shirts were imposed, and the appointment of a spiritual director more reasonable than the first was unable to diminish her folly in the slightest. She remained in this state for four years, and would have stayed in it for ever if a certain act of piety had not drawn her out of it. One of the pieces of advice she had taken from her old teacher included one that she followed with a matchless regularity. She resorted to a painting of Saint Alexis, the mirror of chastity, which was in her oratory, and prostrated herself before it every time she felt lured by temptation, or sensed within herself those movements of which she so frequently accused herself. So one day when she found herself more stirred than usual, and her nature was struggling against her more violently than usual, she resorted to her saint: with tears in her eyes, her face on the ground and her heart borne heavenwards, she told him of the extreme danger in which she found herself, and related, with a marvellous candour and simplicity, how vainly she had fought, and how intently she had striven to suppress the violent transports that she felt.

She accompanied her prayer with penances and lashes of the whip, which she applied to herself in the presence of that blessed pilgrim. But just as it is related of him that he was not affected by the beauty of his wife on his wedding night, and abandoned her, the lovely body of this innocent girl, exposed naked before him, made no impression on his mind, and the lashes with which she belaboured herself so mightily did not induce him to have compassion on her. After lacerating her flesh in this way, she recommended herself again to the handsome Roman, and withdrew herself, as if in victory, to dedicate herself in all tranquillity to less arduous exercises.

AGNÈS – Oh God! Once superstition has gained possession of a soul, how greatly does it ravage it!

ANGÉLIQUE – Hardly had Dosithée left her room than she felt her body all aflame, and her mind drawn to the quest for a pleasure with which she was as yet unacquainted. An extraordinary tingling animated all her senses, and her imagination, filling with a thousand lascivious ideas, left that poor nun half-vanquished. In this pitiful state she returned to her intercessor, redoubled her prayers, and begged him, with the most heartfelt piety one can imagine, to grant her the gift of self-control. Her fervour drove her on; she again picked up her instruments of penitence and availed herself of them for a quarter of an hour with the most distracted and the most indiscreet ardour in the world.

AGNÈS – And... did that give her any relief?

ANGÉLIQUE – Alas! Far from it! She came out of her oratory feeling even more transported with love than before. The bell rang for vespers: she barely managed to stay there all the way through. Sparks of fire were darting from her eyes, and I stared at her without knowing what she was suffering from, but wondering at her restlessness and continual fidgeting.

AGNÈS – What was the reason for it?

ANGÉLIQUE – Well, it was caused by the extreme heat she felt throughout her body, especially in the places to which she had applied the lash. I must tell you that, far from this sort of exercise being able to quench the flames consuming her; her efforts had the opposite effect, and had increased her desires more and more, reducing the poor child to a state in which she could barely stop herself yielding. This is quite understandable, especially since the lashing she had given herself on her backside had excited the heat in all the neighbouring parts, and had borne thither the purest and most subtle spirits of the blood, which, in order to find an exit in conformity with their fiery nature, were sharply pricking the places where they had gathered, as if to force their way out there.

AGNÈS – Did the struggle last for a long time?

ANGÉLIQUE – It began and was ended in a single day. As soon as vespers were finished, as if Dosithée had not been able to address God directly, she went off straightaway to prostrate herself in her oratory. She prays, she weeps, she groans: all in vain. She feels more harassed than ever, and in order to attack her stubborn mature again, she picks up her whip, and lifts up her skirt and her chemise to her navel and, tying it in place with a belt, she violently belabours her buttocks and the parts – all exposed – that are causing her so much torment. Her rage lasted for a while, but then she ran out of strength for this cruel exercise: she was too exhausted even to take off her habit, and so was left half naked. She laid her head on her bed and, reflecting on the condition of men, which she decided was an unhappy one, since they were born with impulses that were condemned even though it was almost impossible to suppress them, she fell into a swoon – but it was an amorous swoon, caused by the fury of her passion, and it enabled this young girl to enjoy a pleasure that swept her up into the heavens. At that moment, nature, uniting all her forces, broke through all the obstacles that had opposed her outbursts, and the virginity which had hitherto lain captive now impetuously yielded itself, being no longer able to defend itself; and it left its guardian stretched out on the ground, in clear token of her defeat.

AGNÈS – Ah! I *so* wish I had been there!

ANGÉLIQUE – Alas! What pleasure would you have had? You would have seen a half-naked, innocent girl uttering cries which she could not explain to herself! You would have seen her in ecstasy, her eyes half-expiring, without strength or vigour, succumbing to the laws of nature most pure, and losing, despite her care, the treasure which she had found it so difficult to preserve.

AGNÈS – Ah now, but that is exactly what I would have enjoyed seeing – gazing at her all naked, and following with a curious eye all the transports which love gave her at the very moment she was vanquished.

ANGÉLIQUE – As soon as Dosithée had recovered from this syncope, her mind, which was before enshrouded in thick darkness, immediately found itself emerging from all its obscurity; her eyes were opened, and, reflecting on what she had done, and on the lack of virtue of the saint on whom she had so intently called, she realised that she had been in a state of error, and, in a surprising metamorphosis rising by her own strength above all the things which she had not heretofore dared to examine, she now despised all the more those which had most held her in their thrall.

AGNÈS – In other words, having been over-punctilious, she now became impious, and no longer sacrificed anything to all the saintikins that she had worshipped before.

ANGÉLIQUE – You are misinterpreting her reaction. One can shed one's superstitions without falling into impiety; this is what Dosithée did. She learned from her experience that it was to the sovereign physician that she needed to resort in her moments of weakness; temptations were not in the power of the faithful to overcome, and in the most submissive soul there often arose involuntary thoughts and impulses which did not comprise even the slightest sin. As you see, I told you nothing but the truth when I assured you that it was piety that had led her away from her over-punctilious conscience.

Something very similar happened to an Italian nun who, having frequently prostrated herself before the figure of a newborn child, whom she called her little Jesus, and having begged it several times to grant her the same thing, in these tender words that she uttered with extraordinary affection: *Dolce signor mio Gesu, fate mi la grazia, etc*,[3] seeing that all her prayers had no effect, she thought that the cause lay in the youthful years of the one she was invoking, and that she would be better off if she addressed the image of the Eternal Father, who represented the Lord at a rather more advanced age. So she went to her little Signor, whom she rebuked for his lack of virtue, protesting that she would never spend her free time with him nor with any child of the same kind, and left him thus, applying to him the words of the proverb: *Chi s'impaccia con fanciulli, con fanciulli si ritrova.* So just think of how far superstition can extend, and to what extremity of folly ignorance sometimes leads us!

AGNÈS – It is true that this example is a sensible proof of that fact, and the simplicity of the nun in question is without equal. Italian women are, however, not considered to be stupid; they are said to have great intelligence, and few things are capable of puzzling them or escaping their powers of penetration.

ANGÉLIQUE – That is true, commonly speaking; but there are always a few who are not as enlightened as the others. Also, it is not always a mark of stupidity to have scruples and doubts. For you need to know, my dear Agnès, that apart from the things of religion there is nothing certain or assured in this world; there is no point of view that can be sustained, and in the usual run of affairs we have merely false and confused ideas of the things that we think we know most perfectly. The truth is still unknown, and all the labour and cunning of men who apply themselves seriously to seeking it have so far been unable to make it appear to us, even though they have often thought they had discovered it.

AGNÈS – But how, then, should we conduct our minds in such a state of general ignorance?

ANGÉLIQUE – In order not be deceived, my child, we must look at the origins of things, envisaging them in their simple nature, and then judging them in accordance with what we see in them. We must above all avoid allowing our reason to follow mere prejudice and to let itself become obsessed by the feelings of other people – feelings which, for the most part, can be no more than opinions. And finally we need to take care lest we are taken in by our eyes and ears, in other words by a thousand external things which are often used to seduce our senses; instead, we should always keep our minds free and unhampered by the stupid ideas and inane maxims with which common folk are infatuated – they run like animals after each and every thing they are presented with, so long as it assumes some pleasing shape.

AGNÈS – I can understand all that, and I even think that we can push your argument a little further, and take in even more of the things that you exclude. It has to be admitted that listening to you is an intense pleasure; even if you were not as young and beautiful as you are, your mind alone would make you worthy of love. Give me a kiss.

ANGÉLIQUE – With all my heart, my dearest friend; I am delighted that you take pleasure in me, and that I have found you so readily disposed to receive the enlightenment that you were lacking. When we have minds that have emerged from the darkness and freed themselves from every sort of anxiety, there is no moment in our lives in which we cannot enjoy some pleasure, and even turn the pains and scruples of others into a subject for our own entertainment. But let us leave all this moral talk, into which I have allowed myself to become sidetracked. Kiss me, my darling; I love you more than my life.

AGNÈS – Well, are your pleased with that?… You do not seem to think that we might be seen here.

ANGÉLIQUE – Oh? And what do we have to fear? Let us retire into this bower, we shall not be seen by anyone. But I am still not sated, there is something uncommon about your kisses; give me a Florentine kiss.

AGNÈS – I think you have gone mad. Does not everyone kiss in the same way? What do you mean by your *Florentine kiss*?

ANGÉLIQUE – Come a little closer and I will show you.

AGNÈS – Oh God! You are setting me all aflame! Ah! This is a lascivious little trick! Pull back, do! Ah! You are holding me so tight! You are devouring me!

ANGÉLIQUE – I need some payment in return for the lessons I am giving you. That is the way people who are really in love with one another kiss, amorously intertwining their tongues between the lips of the beloved: personally I find that there is nothing sweeter or more delicious, when you perform it the right way, and I never have recourse to it without feeling through my whole body an extraordinary tingling and a certain *je ne sais quoi* which I can explain only by telling you that it is a kiss which spreads universally through all the most secret parts of myself, which penetrates into the very depths of my heart, and which I call with some justice *the epitome of the sovereign pleasure*. So? Do you not have anything to say? How was it for you?

AGNÈS – Did I not make myself clear enough when I told you that you were setting me all aflame? But how come you call such caresses a *Florentine kiss*?

ANGÉLIQUE – It is because, among Italian women, the ladies of Florence are considered the most amorous, and they practise the kiss in the manner you received it from me. They derive a singular pleasure from it, and say that they do it in imitation of the dove – an innocent bird – and that they find a certain lascivious and piquant *something* in it, which they do not find and experience in other kisses. I am amazed the Abbot and the Feuillantine did not teach you about it while

I was on retreat, since they have both travelled into Italy, where they apparently made themselves expert in all the most secret practices of love particular to the people of that country.

AGNÈS – I really did have my mind on other things than those simple amorous dallyings when they came to see me, and so I can no longer remember! What I do know is that there was no caress, no foolish little act, to which their fury did not pay attention; but, ah! the pleasure I took in them was so great, and the rapture those transports threw me into so excessive, that I did not have enough freedom of judgement left to reflect.

ANGÉLIQUE – It is true that the sweet moments in which we enjoy that intense pleasure occupy us so much that we are not able to distract ourselves by any application of our memory, nor to draw up, there and then, an *agenda* of all that is happening within ourselves. Nonetheless, I have no doubt but that the Abbot or the Feuillantine pushed their gallantry quite as far as that; after all, apart from the fact that you have a divine mouth, they are perfectly well-appraised of all the sweetest and most alluring manners employed by men capable of passionate love.

AGNÈS – Alas! For persons dedicated to altars, and vowed to chastity, they know only too much!

ANGÉLIQUE – Really, you are pretending to be ironic, and anyone who did not know you would think that you were talking seriously. But shall I tell you what I think? I think that such men can always know more about these matters, but that they could practise them less; for it is certain that, being directors of souls as they are, they must have a perfect acquaintance with both good and evil, so as to discern justly between them, and to exhort us forcefully to pursue and love the one, and to preach to us, with an equal zeal, to shun and hate the other. But this is the opposite of what they actually do, and the bad books from which they draw enlightenment corrupt their will as much as they illumine their understanding.

AGNÈS – I think that you are using those terms wrongly, and that you are forgetting that, among the learned, there is no book that of its nature bears a forbidden title; only the use we make of it means that it is good, bad, or neither.

ANGÉLIQUE – Oh God! I think you must be dreaming to talk like that, and you must agree with me that there are certain books which are worthless from beginning to end, and whose teachings are essentially the opposite of good morals and the practice of virtue. What can you say about the *School for Girls* and that vile *philosophy* in which everything is so flat and insipid, and whose strong arguments can persuade only low and vulgar souls, and touch only those who are already half corrupted, or spontaneously let themselves indulge in every kind of misdemeanour?

AGNÈS – I admit it: *that* particular book can be put back on the shelf with other useless and indeed forbidden things. I would like to make up for the time that I wasted reading it; there is nothing in it which I liked, and I feel it is to be completely condemned. The Abbot who showed it to me gave me another which is almost on the same theme, but it treats it and handles it with much more skill and spirituality.

ANGÉLIQUE. – I know the book you mean; it is no better than the previous one, from the point of view of morals, and although the purity of its style and its easy eloquence are rather agreeable, this does not prevent it from being extremely dangerous, since the fire and brilliance that are, in many passages, so dazzling cannot but help the venom it contains to flow more sweetly, and insinuate it insensibly into all hearts that are in any way susceptible to it: its title is *The Academy of Ladies*, or *The Seven Satyrical Conversations of Aloïsia*. I had it for over a week, and the man who gave it me to read explained its most difficult features to me and helped me understand perfectly all its mysteries. In particular, he interpreted for me these words, found in the seventh conversation, *amori vera lux*,[4] and demonstrated the anagrammatical sense that they conceal under the simple appearance of the inscription of a medal. I think it is this book that you have in mind?

AGNÈS – Sure is. Oh God! How ingeniously this book invents new pleasures for a soul that is sated and jaded! What pointed remarks and spurs does it not use to prick awake the most dormant, the most languishing lust – even when it can do no more! What extravagant appetites! What strange objects of desire, and what unknown meats it presents! But I can see that I am still less expert than you are in these matters.

ANGÉLIQUE – Alas, my child! The knowledge after which you aspire can only be prejudicial to you. The pleasures on which we are intent need to be kept within their limits by *laws*, by *nature*, and by *prudence*, and all the maxims which this book could teach you all almost equally deviate from these three things. Believe me, all extremes are dangerous, and there is a certain *juste milieu* that we cannot leave without falling into the precipice. *Let us love*, for it is not forbidden; *let us seek pleasure*, so long as it is legitimate; but let us avoid anything that is inspired by the spirit of debauchery alone, and do not let us be seduced by the persuasions of an eloquence that delights us only to destroy us, and which expresses itself in fine words only in order to lead us more easily to commit evil.

Agnès – Oh, what a fine moral lesson! And how well you know to gild the pill when you want to! It is not that I do not bow to your arguments, and do not view all the things that you condemn as wrong; but I cannot help laughing when I see you preaching reformation with so much fire, and when I hear you talking to the deaf and the blind – as are our senses, which refuse to accept any rules other than those which they propose to themselves.

Angélique – That is true, and I admit that it is a bad – I mean useless – employment of one's time to strive to suppress vice and elevate virtue, amid the corruption of the century in which we find ourselves. The malady is too great and the contagion too universal for them to be remedied by mere words, and for these ills to be cured by a mechanism that can act on the mind alone. That is far from being my intention; I was merely very glad to have the opportunity of informing you that you I do not approve of the libertinage of those who never enjoy their pleasures perfect unless they seek them out in the lessons of a corrupt imagination – I mean an imagination which goes beyond the most inviolable limits of nature, and even indulges in the most dissolute licentiousness of the fables of the past.

I am no enemy of sensual delight, nor am I attached to that uncomfortable virtue of which our century is not even capable; and I know that the noblest soul cannot be mistress of her passions, nor purged of other human infirmities, so long as she is still attached to our body.

Agnès – Ah, now I like this change of direction, and this reasonable indulgence is acceptable. For whatever can one find wrong in pleasure when it is kept under control? Something must necessarily be granted to the temperament of the body, and the weakness of our minds must be treated with compassion, since we receive them just as nature gives them to us, and it is not within our power to choose them. We are not responsible for the fantasies produced by the leanings and inclinations that nature gives us. If they are failings, it is she who is guilty of them, she who is blameworthy, and men cannot be reproached for the vices which are born with them, or which proceed from their birth alone.

ANGÉLIQUE – You are right, my darling, and I cannot express the joy that I feel when these words enable me to see the progress that, under my guidance, you have made. But let us not rack our minds any longer delving into the crimes of others; let us tolerate what we cannot reform, and let us not try to alter evils that would no doubt reveal all too clearly the powerlessness of our remedies. Let us live for ourselves and not fall ill with infirmities we catch from others; let us establish within ourselves that peace and that spiritual tranquillity that is the principle of joy, and the beginning of the happiness that we can reasonably desire.

AGNÈS – For my part, I am already peacefully relishing that repose and quietude of spirit, which I have reached, I dare say, only thanks to you. I have obligations to you that I will never be able to acknowledge as much as I would like; after all, for all the pains you have taken to draw me out of the error in which I was languishing, you are content with the friendship that I have sworn to you – may it replace any other reward you may deserve!

ANGÉLIQUE – Alas, my child! What could you offer me that would please me any more greatly? I prefer your caresses to all the treasures of the world; a single one of your kisses enchants me and overwhelms me with its riches. But look, there is someone coming; let us go our separate ways so as to prevent them forming any suspicions as to our conversations. Kiss me, my dear child.

AGNÈS. – I will, with a *Florentine kiss*.

ANGÉLIQUE – Ah, you ravish me! You transport me! Enough, I beg you! You are giving me countless pleasures.

AGNÈS – That is enough for the present. Farewell, Angélique. Sister Cornélie is approaching.

ANGÉLIQUE – I can see her. She doubtless wishes to give me some order from Madame. Farewell, Agnès! Farewell, my heart, my delight, my love!

FOURTH CONVERSATION
SISTER AGNÈS, SISTER ANGÉLIQUE

AGNÈS – Ah, good day, Angélique; how are you?

ANGÉLIQUE – Very well, thank God; I am delighted to see you; I was thinking of you just now.

AGNÈS – Oh? What were you thinking about?

ANGÉLIQUE – I was thinking of coming to enjoy myself in your company, and to tell you the news that I have learned from Sister Cornélie.

AGNÈS – What have you learned? Did you clearly recognise her?

ANGÉLIQUE – To be honest, when she came into my room, I did not recognise her, since I took her to be a person of high quality, because she seemed to have two pages in her suite, and was accompanied by a very handsome gentleman who was talking to her.

AGNÈS – So you eventually did recognise her?

ANGÉLIQUE – Yes, both from her words and from her gestures, and also from several other things that completely convinced me that it was she.

AGNÈS – So then, tell me, who was the gentleman accompanying her?

ANGÉLIQUE – It was the Marquis de Gracio, a native of Florence, a very fine figure of a man, very richly dressed.

AGNÈS – Tell met the news that Sister Cornélie told you, and make it quick!

ANGÉLIQUE – I will tell you the story. Sister Cornélie is to marry Frédéric, who is a young man from a very decent family, a very handsome fellow. I could draw a portrait of him for you, but I will tell you frankly that I prefer to depict our own sex than that of men.

Agnès – Oh? Why is that? Is there such a difference between men and us? Since you will not describe or depict the features of a man for me, give me a portrait of Sister Cornélie; it has been a long time since I saw her, and I do not even know if I would recognise her.

Angélique – Ah, sister Agnès, of course I will, and with all my heart! I can tell you that she is quite tall, and has an elegant way of walking; she has a lovely body, her flesh is firm and white as ivory, and soft to the touch; she is neither thin nor fat; she has a fine cleavage, and her breasts are round and not far from her stomach; she is tightly belted and broad of haunch; she does not have a single wrinkle on her face; on the contrary, it is smooth all over; her arms are rounded, her hands of middling length and slender, her thighs plump, her knees small, her legs beautiful and straight – in short, she is wonderfully well appointed right down to her heels, which are joined to tiny, shapely feet. Finally, apart from all the beauties that nature has given her, she has a great number of the fine qualities that are a girl's greatest charms.

Agnès – To tell you the truth, I was right to say that I would not recognise her, since it seems to me that she did not used to have all those qualities, nor those perfections of body. From the way you are depicting her, it cannot be the same girl.

Angélique – I admit that I found she had changed a great deal; but after all, the company that people keep can change them considerably, especially those of our sex, when they take the trouble to correct all their clumsiness and other failings.

Agnès – Finally, Sister Cornélie is to marry Frédéric, then?

Angélique – Yes.

Agnès – Tell me, is it the same Frédéric whom I met six years ago in Florence, at the house of the Count d'Arnobio?

Angélique – The same – and I can swear to you, as a friend,

that I take as much joy in it, and participate as closely, as if I were to share alone in the first pleasures.

AGNÈS – I am delighted that Sister Cornélie came to visit you, for she has given us an opportunity to converse on this subject awhile.

ANGÉLIQUE – Actually, apart from all the perfections of body and qualities she possesses, she is also particularly expert in history and foreign languages. Everyone soon realises that she knows the most hidden things of nature – all thanks to the liveliness of her mind.

AGNÈS – You surprise me, Angélique; I can hardly believe what you are telling me about Sister Cornélie.

ANGÉLIQUE – Alas! You still do not know half the things that Sister Cornélie told me. To converse further on this point, I can tell you that Frédéric went to visit her, among others, and found her entirely naked in her room. She turned round and said to him with a smile, 'What do you want?' He replied, 'Ah! my sweetheart! My sole pleasure of Venus!' After these words, she put on her chemise, and went over to him. Then he immediately placed his hand on that marble column; she, filled with surprise, replied to him, 'Are you not ashamed to hold me like that?' All her words were in vain; for he embraced her with an extraordinary ardour, telling her, 'Kiss me, my beloved.' No sooner had he kissed her than he pushed her down onto the bed and started furiously fondling her breasts, her nipples, etc, kissing her more and more fiercely, telling her, 'Did you think that you could enjoy such pleasure without men?' After they had enjoyed to the full several particular pleasures, I think he kissed her over a thousand times, and as a result, before daybreak, they redoubled this sweet pastime over three times. I also believe that they promised each other to reiterate it on several subsequent nights; but that is what I am not sure of, being unable to hear everything they said, as I was afraid of being seen by them. Then Sister Cornélie acknowledged that such pleasure came indeed from conjunction with a man.

AGNÈS – Oh? How did you find all this out? Sister Cornélie must have told you, or you must have seen and heard them through a crack, and I even think there must have been a torch lit in the room.

ANGÉLIQUE – You are right, I did see a light, and noticed an image of Our Lady, in front of whom Sister Cornélie was accustomed to say her prayers every evening before going to bed. I can also tell you, Sister Agnès, that I saw Sister Cornélie, completely naked, looking for bugs in her chemise (it was July) and Frédéric next to her, bent at the waist, holding in his hand… which greatly surprised me, since I had imagined she could not possibly have enjoyed as much pleasure as she claimed.

And I said to myself, 'Alas! How Sister Cornélie must have suffered! How can he not have hurt her?' That is how I spoke to myself; then I concluded: 'He must have treated her very gently because of her youth' – since she cannot have been more than fifteen. Filled with amazement, I heard her crying out in pain, and I even thought she was going to die, which greatly bothered me – I did not dare enter the room, for fear of causing them distress. However, a few moments later, I saw her embrace Frédéric in both arms with considerable intensity and friendship.

Frédéric responded with equal fervour, saying, 'Ah! The pleasure I enjoy with you!' In short, by demonstrating such warmth of emotion for each other, followed by sighs and groans, they took their rest and remained for a while both in a swoon. As evidence of the excessive love that Sister Cornélie bore Frédéric, I can tell you that, in spite of her swoon, she started to kiss him – to kiss him all over, not to put too fine a point on it; and she talked to him in the sweetest terms imaginable, from whence I concluded that she had enjoyed real pleasure. This filled me with a longing to enjoy a similar pleasure, and I can even tell you that the idea almost drove me out of my mind. Thinking of it all night, I could not sleep until the morning; luckily fortune, which was quite favourable to my desires, brought me some relief. It was the elder son of Count Don Gracio, who, as luck would have it, chanced to set his eyes on me and started to love me: every time that I saw him, I could not help but reciprocate his love. We both started with amorous gazes, then we greeted each other with bows and then by word of mouth; afterwards, by providing the most particular proof of friendship and love; but what annoyed me was that, at the height of our pleasures, I was obliged to change rooms, which saddened me considerably; however, this did not prevent him from cunningly ensuring that I received from him a letter in which he assured me that he was burning with love for me, and begged me to take pity on him by responding to his passion and his flame. You can imagine with what a shudder (of love, I mean) I read that letter; I thought I would faint away with desire and my only thought was now of enjoying my dear Don Gracio. With this in mind, I replied to him that he should come to me as soon as possible; that I would grant him all that he could hope for from a girl who loved him more than she did her own life, and that I would do everything in my power to find myself in the first room, so as better to enjoy the pleasures that I expected from him. No sooner had he received this agreeable news than he set out to visit me. I had prepared myself to receive him, and bring him into a suitable room next to that of Sister Cornélie, and here we would give each other proofs of our love. It so happened that he was lucky enough to find, a few yards away from our rooms, our servant Madelon, who (luckily for me) was at that time my good friend and confidante, and from her he learned of my yearning to enjoy the height of pleasure with him; she showed him the door through which he could enter. She also came to inform me, with a great deal of joy, of her encounter with Don Gracio, and told me that he wished to find out from me how and when he might enter without being seen by anyone; to which request I replied most rapidly, telling her to pass on to him the information that the door by which he usually came in to see me would be half-open, and that I would wait for him all alone, reposing on a bed of damask; if he loved me, I hoped that he would not make me wait too long – for I am impatient once I have arranged a tryst. He arrived at about half-past eleven. I was very happy to see him. I have to admit that the first embrace filled me with a degree of fear, not because of the darkness, but because I had not been expecting to see him so soon, and his arrival seized me, not with anxiety, but with joy. Finally, however, my panic soon subsided. His kisses and all his caresses showed me that I was about to become the happiest girl in the world. My modesty, struggling against my exorbitant love, made me receive his first caresses, which were merely a beginning, with a certain sense of inner shame; but shortly afterwards I responded in a way he was not expecting. That is why, having thrown me onto the bed, he kissed me again a million times over. I sustained this amorous play as a true child of Venus, and we returned to it more than once, but with much more excellent pleasures, as he gave me kisses that would have made the gods jealous. 'Ah! how these embraces are filled with tenderness! How agreeable and delightful it is to fondle you thus! Allow me to place my mouth between these two breasts' (this is how he spoke), 'and let me cover with my one hand this sacred mount of Love and Venus, and with the other hand touch those firm white buttocks!'

AGNÈS – Ah, Angélique! It is so enchanting to talk to you! I would prefer such pleasures to my condition, if I were as expert as you in this domain.

ANGÉLIQUE – The following day, at the same time, we continued these same frolics, and in the same way, with the most amorous combats, although our pleasures would as yet remain quite imperfect (or so he told me) unless I remedied my shortcomings. 'But,' I told him, 'you would be right to complain about me if my fault did not proceed from ignorance; for I am by nature more inclined to compassion than cruel or insensitive to the pains and pleasures of others, and particularly of those I love. So I beg you,' I told him, 'to pardon my simplicity; I hope that, with time, I will provide what we are still lacking in order to enjoy our pleasures with greater comfort.' Having said these words, I wanted to leave, so that I could teach myself about this subject by reading a few books that treat of the matter, but he held me by my skirt, begging that we immediately return to our caresses, and demonstrate the violent love that we had for each other, before we said goodbye. He made me lie on my side on the bed, and came to lie next to me as you can imagine, and swore that he loved me more than his own life, and I proclaimed that I cherished him just as much; as a result, once both of us had made these protestations of friendship, we had to start all over again with our kisses, embraces, and fondlings and ticklings – all of which filled us with extreme contentment.

AGNÈS – Well, are you indeed content? Is your curiosity fully satisfied now that you have lost – as I conclude from what you have been telling me – your virginity? But tell me, I beg you, Angélique – did not Don Gracio run the risk of falling ill after toiling away for so long?

ANGÉLIQUE – Our servant went for a walk and happened to meet Catherine, the servant of Don Gracio, who told her of the misfortune that had befallen her master. She told me, in accents of great sadness and sorrow, that Don Gracio had a violent fever that had laid him low. You can easily imagine how much this news afflicted me, as well as our servant. She went off to carry out her tasks, and I meditated on the means of repairing such a great loss, for I was told that he was in great danger of dying, seeing how violent his fever was. And so it turned out.

AGNÈS – So – no more Gracio for you?

ANGÉLIQUE – True. Too bad: I have found a replacement. One holiday, on a visit to Mme the Abbess de Flori, I saw Samuel arriving in the same town. He looked really very tired: when I spotted him, I followed him and saw him enter the same room where he had stayed a year or two ago. As soon as he went in, he merely pushed open the door, without closing it behind him, and sat down on the bed; and this led me to say to myself, 'Alas! The poor boy, he is without a woman, just as I am without Don Gracio. I can see that he is longing to out what heaven has given him to use. What!' I said, 'and why do I not go to him? If he needs anything, why should I not content him?' This is what I said to myself. 'And there is nobody with him.'

AGNÈS – Is he a person young in age and handsome of body?

ANGÉLIQUE – Samuel is about twenty to twenty-one, and of ordinary height. His hair is the colour of gold, his eyes are very amorous, his face very handsome, and his legs are very shapely. After gazing my fill at him through the door, as before on all the occasions when we have met, (I have known him for two years), I resolved, all trembling, to knock on the door, but love overwhelmed my fear and led me to enter in quite boldly, without waiting for him to come and open the door. He seemed to be more ashamed than I was at this sudden irruption. I went over to his bed, smiling but saying nothing, and he asked me, taking my left hand and turning it in his, 'Well, Angélique! My sweetheart, my love, what is all this about?' Then he pulled me and threw me down on the bed next to him, staring at my breasts with eyes so soulful and inflamed that I suspected something; that is why I jumped out of bed to go and close and lock the door and block the holes in it; then, having returned to the bed, I said to him, in rather affected tomes, 'Samuel, I am taking this precaution because there is something particular I would like to say to you…' Whereupon, interrupting me, he wanted… 'Ah!' I said to him, 'Samuel, what are you up to? Hands off!'

AGNÈS – So, seems as if you were pretending that sugar would not melt in your mouth. I foretold such encounters a long time ago, and I am never wrong. Do not men have the right, as much as we do, to seek what they like, so as to enjoy a few pleasures? And you well know that our hearts cannot get by without a little amusement; in any case, nature allows these hearts of ours to seek out objects that will fulfil them, and attach themselves to people for whom we feel friendship.

ANGÉLIQUE – And yet I have seen people who condemned that freedom as a great crime.

AGNÈS – I can well believe it: it is true that civil laws are in this regard contrary to the laws of nature, but this is merely to avoid the licentiousness that might spread through the world.

Admittedly, in the commerce of love, one needs to avoid publicity; otherwise, divulging one's activities to all and sundry would be extremely imprudent. You can play the hypocrite, pull a few faces at the right time and place, speak little, and even refrain from showing any passion to the person you love, as well as making the most of the twilight hour when lovers meet their loves. These are the means used also by the women who wish to live happily within the servitude of marriage, by hiding the mysteries of their hearts, and planting horns in abundance on their husbands' heads, without those poor husbands even realising. This is the way we need to govern ourselves, both the virgins and the women among us.

ANGÉLIQUE – You surprise me, Agnès, by the ease with which you could deceive a man, if you ever had one; you speak of it as authentically as if you had already had experience of it. Your whole attitude will not lead me to turn away from Samuel just like that, nor even from a husband; if I had one, I would love him too much to make him wear a crown of horns.

AGNÈS – Alas, Angélique! If you still possessed your virginity, one might believe that you were altogether innocent in this business. Do you not know that people weary of always eating the same morsel? Change, for us, is usually a tasty and appetising ragout; indeed, there are few women (none, actually) who do not resort to change when they find an opportunity; so imagine what those women do who have (or so they say) only one gallant – and how they govern themselves!

ANGÉLIQUE – I still have to tell you that all your words will not persuade me and that I am of a mind to remain faithful to Samuel. But tell me: what are the reasons that are impelling you to dissuade me away from Samuel?

AGNÈS – Oh, how stubborn you are! I ask you! Who else could turn insurmountable necessity into a reason for moral obloquy! If it is merely the fates that give us such a violent inclination, how ever can we avoid succumbing? Neither Minerva herself, nor all the vestals, can resist it.

ANGÉLIQUE – You are importuning me so insistently on this matter that I am going to change the subject. Well now: one day, I received a visit from Rodolphe, who was accompanied by a lady of quality; her name is Alios. She was wearing a great deal of taffeta, tricked out with a number of ribbons of many colours, admirably well-matched. Her breast was covered with a very fine and slender gauze, which she was wearing as the weather was mild and serene; through it there appeared two shapely globes, and her mouth, as she opened it, showed two rows of dazzling white teeth – but it was her curly blond hair, in particular, fluttering all around her polished brow with its alabaster hue, that added such lustre to her loveliness and grace, and the love that shone in her face. She did me the honour of singing several lovely songs, with agreeable roulades, admirably paced. She produced a sweet harmony to which Rodolphe and I gave all our attention, trying to learn the songs by heart, Rodolphe in particular; but the sight of him, which moreover was having an effect on her person just as much as on myself, destroyed this enterprise. In this feast for ears and eyes, Rodolphe struck up a friendship with Alios (this was indeed what he was seeking, since the familiarity between the two of them was not yet intense enough), begging her to be so kind as to permit him to give himself the honour and allow that he might be granted the advantage of seeing her sometimes, hoping that this would not be refused him, and believing that he was not in the bad books of her father, as well as in hers, continuing to tell her that conversing with her was sweet and agreeable; indeed, if he dared, he would take the liberty one day of going to visit her in her house in the country, where he knew that she was to spend several holidays, counting that day – he said – among his happiest, for he hoped so much charity from her person that she would be so kind as to grant him this favour; which she did, and received him with an especial joy, as you can well imagine. Finally, he went to visit her in that pleasure ground that can be called the Palace of Pleasure; not for the neat attractions that he could find there, but because, in the presence of Alios, his mind was fed by a thousand amorous pleasures and even though he almost did not dare to communicate with her – because of her father, of whom, as you know, he was rather afraid – other than by cunning little stratagems, he nonetheless flattered himself with hope, thinking that time would give birth to happier moments.

AGNÈS – Did he not say anything else to her? Did he not speak of a few particular pleasures? I am most afraid, Angélique, that you are not telling me everything.

ANGÉLIQUE – You are being malicious, as I can see; I will tell you some other time about all that pertains to this subject; every thing in due season. I will merely tell you that I beg all the gods and all the goddesses, in a word all the divinities who have been sensible to love, to be present, and to protect Rodolphe in all his enterprises.

AGNÈS – Apparently, Rodolphe is a good friend of yours, and I can see that you would like him to bring his endeavours to a completion. There is no reason for me to tell you every-thing that I think about Rodolphe and you. I will simply say that I think he has given you a few of Venus's pleasures.

ANGÉLIQUE – Ah, I think you are mocking me when you talk like that! Just listen to the story I am going to tell you of my meeting. So anyway: in the morning, as soon as I had risen, and dressed myself in a new habit that I had had made for myself for holy days, Alios and I went to Father Théodore's, after we had said our prayers. You will recognise who I mean when I tell you that he is one of those men who affect an apparent austerity of life and a quite unusual severity of morals: I can also tell you that every sermon is for them (I think you understand these terms) mortification and penitence; and the beards which they grow, making their faces thin and hollowed, lead the people to imagine that they are true mirrors of sanctity. 'Well, my dear girl!' he said, going up to her, 'you have a father who will spare nothing to render you as perfect as you must needs be. From what he told me, you are soon to be married to Rodolphe; so you must cleanse your soul of every stain in order to render yourself worthy of the grace of heaven, which cannot enter into a heart sullied by the least trace of pollution. You need to know,' he continued, 'that if you are pure, the children who spring from the marriage and whom you bring into the world will, one day, in heaven fill the places of the rebel angels; but on the contrary, if you have any bad quality, they will be infected, and will follow the path of perdition to increase the number of those wretches. It is for you' – he told her – 'to choose.' She was so filled with shame that she did not dare to reply. 'Speak, speak,' he said. 'I would like,' she told him, 'to be purified, and my children to be good.' There was in the same room as Father Théodore a Reverend

Jesuit Father who, after listening to the conversation between Father Théodore and Alios for some time, went away – which Alios was not displeased at, since she was then emboldened to talk to Théodore more frankly, and made her confession to him, down to the least thought of sin of which she thought herself guilty. When he learned, among other things, what had occurred between Rodolphe and her, and that she had already half-tasted the pleasures which love inspires, he very nearly flew into a rage. He reprimanded her severely, after warning her to view her previous actions with horror; then he gave to Alios's father, without unfolding it, a small bundle of cords that he drew from his sleeve.[5] 'Go,' he said, 'and do not spare your daughter, but serve as an example to her, and do not think yourself too indulgent.' After that, we left Father Théodore's room and came back to my room.

AGNÈS – Do you not marvel, Angélique, how those people deceive our simple minds? I imagine that Alios believes him as gospel truth, just like her father?

ANGÉLIQUE – As if we were bothered! No sooner had we reached my room than Alios's father closed the door, and with a laugh gave his daughter Alios the bundle of cords to unwrap – which she did; I easily recognised it to be a kind of whip (for I had seen other examples before) composed of five cordlets, knotted with countless little knots spaced out all along it. 'Well, my daughter!' he said, 'it is with this instrument of piety, as the Church calls it, that you must dispose yourself for marriage, since you have a desire to marry; it must serve you as a purgation. The good Father,' he continued, 'has ordered us both to chastise ourselves: I will start,' he said, 'and you will follow me; but do not let the vigour with which I treat my body alarm you; do not be afraid, and just remember, as I will, that during this holy exercise of piety, my spirit will be tasting sweet and inexpressible joys.'

AGNÈS – Alios trembled, no doubt, to hear her father saying such things?

ANGÉLIQUE – No, and I must admit that I did not think that she could have such strength as to tolerate, as she did, that harsh and painful travail.

AGNÈS – Indeed, they say that there is nobody more constant and stubborn than that girl, once she has determined to endure some pain. She overcomes herself, tolerating with admirable firmness pains that would weary the bravest men in the world; I think it is doubtless the love she bears Rodolphe that inspires her to suffer this harsh exercise. But continue, Angélique, and tell me of the holy exercise ordered by Father Théodore.

ANGÉLIQUE – Well, one of Alios's aunts arrived by chance in the room just as Alios and her father were about to embark on their exercise. This aunt, who is a real bigot, wanted to take Alios's father's place, saying that it was not the custom for men to perform such tasks, and that, in her view, there was much greater glory in putting oneself in somebody else's place to execute the orders of good Father Théodore: and this she immediately did, undressing herself down to her chemise, which she lifted up to her shoulders; then, sinking to her knees, and picking up the whip I mentioned, she said, 'Look, my niece, how one should use this instrument of penance, and learn to suffer from the example I am about to give you.' Hardly had she finished speaking than I heard someone knocking at the door; I alerted her. 'I know who it is,' said Alios's father, 'it is good Father Théodore, who has doubtless come to help us in this holy exercise; he had told me that he would not miss it, if he could obtain permission to come out.' He knocked a second time. 'It is indeed he,' repeated Alios's father. 'Go,' he said to his daughter, 'open the door for him straightaway.'

'What?' replied Alios, 'do you want him to see my aunt completely naked?'

'So,' said the father to his daughter, 'you do not know that this holy man has seen right into your aunt's innermost soul, and that nothing should be hidden from him?'

But Alios's aunt did lower her chemise while her niece went to let him in. Father Théodore immediately came in and praised Alios's aunt for the good example she had set her niece; he then gave a speech on this subject, but with such force and energy that Alios almost stopped him to beg him to treat her with as much vigour as he could.

AGNÈS – Ah God! Is it possible? Was Alios so crazy? Was she so simpleminded and so bigoted?

ANGÉLIQUE – You would have found it difficult not to yield, and he would doubtless have persuaded you. He proved to them, by a polished speech, apparently prepared in advance, that virginity, in mortification and penitence, was in no way meritorious; that it was merely a dry and sterile virtue, and that if it were not accompanied by some voluntary chastisement, there was nothing more vile, and even contemptible. 'Doubtless,' he continued, 'those women who show themselves naked to men, so as to prostitute themselves to their lusts, should blush with shame; but on the contrary, those who do so merely out of a principle of piety and penitence, and even out of a holy zeal for the purification of their souls, should be praised. If you consider the action of the former,' he said, continuing to speak, 'you will find that it is altogether foul, and if you look then at the other, you will see that it encloses within itself every kind of honest virtue; the one can satisfy mortals alone, but the other is capable of enchanting the gods. Above all,' he continued, 'these sorts of chastisements are of great use when you know when to resort to them; they are like a divine spring whose miraculous waters have the virtue of cleansing women from all the filth they might have contracted; women have no means of purging themselves other than by suffering with as much firmness and patience the penance that is imposed on them, once they have sensually tasted the pleasures that were forbidden them.' Finally, he told them that in this way their souls were cleansed of countless sins and crimes that shame and modesty often prevented them from revealing when they needed forgiveness.

AGNÈS – Oh, what a fine moral sense he has! Ah, how alluring these precepts are! Apparently, from what he said, he has performed this sacred task several times?

ANGÉLIQUE – After all these speeches, Agnès, he took his whip in his hand; Alios's aunt went down on her knees and Alios withdrew some distance, her eyes still fixed on her aunt. Having thus adopted the right posture, she begged Father Théodore to start his holy work (that was the term she used). Hardly had she uttered the last word than a hail of lashes fell on her completely naked bottom; then he whipped her a little less severely, but he finally reduced her to such a state that her buttocks, which had been very white and polished beforehand, became as red as fire; the sight of them, indeed, inspired horror.

AGNÈS – Oh? And she did not complain?

ANGÉLIQUE – Far from it; she seemed insensible, and uttered a sigh just once, saying, 'Ah! My Father!' But this (self-proclaimed) executor of divine justice grew angry. 'Where then is your courage?' he said to her. 'You really are setting a fine example of weakness to your niece!' He then ordered her to bend her head and body down to the earth, which she did, and never had she presented such a lovely spectacle. Her buttocks were so exposed to the lashes that not one missed its mark; this lasted for a quarter of an hour or thereabouts; after which the good Father said to her, 'That is enough, get up; your spirit must be content'. She rose, and went over to her niece: 'Well, my niece!' she said embracing her, 'now it is your turn to show that you have courage'.

'I hope,' replied Alios, 'that I will not be lacking in it.'

'What must I do?' said Alios's aunt to Father Théodore.

'Prepare your niece,' said the good Father, 'I hope that she will be even stronger and more courageous than you.'

However, Alios's eyes were lowered and she said nothing.

'Are you not going to do as I purposed?' Father Théodore asked her.

'I will at least try,' she said.

During this exchange, her aunt was undressing her down to her chemise, which she lifted up over her shoulders. As soon as she felt herself all naked, modesty and shame covered her face: she started to sink to her knees.

'That is not necessary,' said her aunt; 'stay standing.'

At the same moment Father Théodore broke in.

'Well, Alios, do you want to be happy? Do you want me to set you on the right path to heaven?'

'I wish you would,' she replied.

After these words, he gave her a few lashes, but so gently that he ticked her rather than hurting her.

'Could you, my dear child,' he asked her, 'endure any harsher lashes?'

Her aunt replied for her, and said that she would not be lacking in courage, and that he needed merely to pursue his holy exercise. Immediately, from top to bottom, Alios felt herself belaboured with lashes, but of such violence that she could not stop herself crying, 'Ah! Ah! Ah! Enough! Enough! Have pity on me, my aunt!'

'Take courage,' she replied. 'Do you want to want to finish what is left of this exercise, so holy and so good – this purgative for the most begrimed souls?'

'Very well,' said Father Théodore; 'let us see how she spares herself. Take,' he continued, 'this holy instrument of penitence, and chastise as you should that part of the body which is the seat of vile pleasure.'

Her aunt showed her with her hand what to do. Alios gave herself five or six moderately harsh lashes, but she could not continue. 'I cannot,' she said to her aunt, 'I cannot hurt myself; if you wish, I am prepared to suffer all from you.'

So saying, she handed her the whip; and her aunt in turn gave it to Father Théodore, 'Since,' she said, 'you will gain more merit if you endure chastisement from him rather than from someone else.' He immediately started to whip Alios, murmuring between his teeth I know not what prayer. She was weeping, she was sighing, and at every lash he gave, she wriggled her buttocks strangely. Finally he wore her down so much that she could resist no longer: she ran from one side of the room to the other to escape the lashes.

'I cannot stand it any more,' she repeated; 'this travail exceeds my strength.'

'Say rather,' replied Father Théodore, 'that you are a coward and a heartless girl; are you not ashamed to be the niece of such a good and courageous aunt, and to behave in such a weak manner?'

'Obey,' her aunt told her.

'I consent,' said Alios, 'do with me what you will.'

At these words, her aunt immediately bound her hands with a small slender cord, since she had been warding off with her hands many of the lashes; then she laid her down on the bed, where she was given a good thrashing. While Father Théodore whipped her, her aunt kept kissing her, saying, 'Courage, my niece, this holy work will soon be finished, and the more lashes you take, the more merit you will have.'

'Finally,' said the Father, 'that is good: the victim has shed enough blood for the sacrifice to be agreeable.'

AGNÈS – Ah God! What a sacrifice, what butchery and what a torturer!

ANGÉLIQUE – But Agnès, what can we do about it? It is a maxim that has prevailed in every age. Once it had been completed, her aunt unbound her arms, praising her volubly for having suffered so patiently a travail so harsh for a girl like her. The Father immediately spoke a few very kindly words to her as he went off, giving her his blessing. As soon as he had gone, her aunt embraced her with a great deal of tenderness. 'You need, my niece,' she said, 'to pretend to be ill with a pain in your side, so as to take the rest that is necessary to you. As for me,' she continued, 'I am accustomed to these sorts of exercises, and I am no longer discommoded by them. Farewell, until tomorrow.'

AGNÈS – Do you know what she did during the time she was alone in her room?

ANGÉLIQUE – Yes. She went to amuse herself, after resting for a while, by reading some very fine books; here is a list of them:

Scaramouche's Religion.

The Reformed Whore, illustrated.

The Overthrowing of the Convents, a curious play.

The Languishing Vatican.

A Conversation Between the Pope and the Devil,
in burlesque verse.

The Monopoly of Purgatory.

The Devil Disfigured, illustrated.

The Genealogy of the Marquis de Arana.

Robert's Sauce, a curious play.

The Policies of the Jesuits.

Truly, Agnès, are these not fine books? We can only conclude that she found great entertainment in reading these
books. If you ask me, given their titles, I cannot imagine that
they were anything other than most curious.

AGNÈS – Ah, how happy she would have been, and how
content, if destiny had granted her to enjoy the embraces of
Rodolphe! I think that if Alios had known then where
Rodolphe was, or if Rodolphe had managed to find out
where Alios was, he would have used that time well.

ANGÉLIQUE – He did, however, suspect something; that is why
fortune, which has always been favourable to him, made
him come to the room where Alios was; he found her lying
on her bed; she was pretending to be asleep; he flung his
arms around her, he kissed her and fondled different parts
of her body; she, for her part, took him by a place – ah!
I dare not say it! – which he could not resist. What more
would you have wanted, if you had been in her place? You
can imagine the rest.

AGNÈS – But tell me, how have you been able to find out things
which doubtless occurred in secret? Alios must have related
all these details to you – or were you always in her company?

ANGÉLIQUE – She herself confided in me, and told me everything, down to the last words; apart from that, I found
myself several times with her, and witnessed various things
that happened to her.

AGNÈS – It has to be admitted, Angélique, that you have
derived a great deal of pleasure from this. You must be really
satisfied.

ANGÉLIQUE – You are right; there is only this custom of
pleasure-seeking that brings people such intense delight.
If the truths which I have related to you were known by
a countless number of punctilious women, they would soon
abandon their foolish opinions and, examining natural
necessities by the rule of a right reason, they would find in
life much more sweetness than they actually experience. To
live happy in this world, we women need to remove all the
prejudices from our minds, excommunicating from them
all that the tyranny of a bad custom may have imprinted in
them, and then to bring our lives into conformity with what
nature, which is entirely pure and innocent, requires of us.

AGNÈS – I am most obliged to you, Angélique, since without
you I would still be in a state of blindness and innocence;
for the effort made by my first acquaintances, the violence
of bad habits, and the torrent of the multitude would
doubtless have swept me away, if the solid education you
have given me had not led me to change my feelings, by
showing me, as you did, the truth.

ANGÉLIQUE – You have forgotten to tell me whether you
approved of this conjunction and this pleasure, or whether
you loathe it as I do?

AGNÈS – I would be wrong to approve it, and even if I did not
speak a word about it, the thunderous voice of Heaven
would condemn me if I did approve it. I will just add this

before I finish. Lucien discusses these two points ingeniously; he does not condemn either, and it is even difficult to say which of the two he prefers. Several other writers seem to share his feelings; but what amazes me is that no lawmaker has forbidden them: on the contrary, they approve every imaginable way of taking pleasure.

ANGÉLIQUE – Oh heavens! I am in despair! Assuredly people have been listening to us, for I have just heard someone on the steps. But come what may, we are not tongue-tied stammerers; denials do not cost so dear these days, and we can provide those who might make so bold as to use this conversation against us with more and to spare.

AGNÈS – You never grow weary of talking, and you have not noticed that the day will soon be over. Let us put off what we have to say until another time. Kiss me, my sweetheart.

ANGÉLIQUE – Ah, Agnès! I will never grow weary of talking with you, I find it so sweet and agreeable. I could spend whole nights doing so and never grow bored. I imagine that you must be as satisfied with my company as I am with yours. Only with pain and sorrow do I ever leave you.

AGNÈS – Ah, how strong you are! I think you will never finish. Farewell.

FIFTH CONVERSATION
SISTER ANGÉLIQUE, SISTER AGNÈS

ANGÉLIQUE – Ah, how glad I am to join you again, my dear Agnès.

AGNÈS – I have been looking for you for a long time, my divine Angélique.

ANGÉLIQUE – Come, let me kiss you, my tender baby.

AGNÈS – If you continue to caress me with such force, you will reduce me to ashes, for I feel myself already all aflame. Leave off, I beg you, from your embraces, and let us continue our conversations, since we are in a suitable spot for that.

ANGÉLIQUE – Gladly; that is why I was looking for you; and yet one should always pay friendship its tribute; so kiss me again.

AGNÈS – Let us make the most of the time, I beg you, lest someone catches us here, or our Abbess, who has her eye on everything, as you know, notices our long and frequent conversations, and orders us, as a penance, to see each other only at services and in the refectory.

ANGÉLIQUE – As far as today is concerned, I can tell you she is unlikely to pay us any attention; she has other things on her mind; she went to see her lady prisoner, or rather her gentleman prisoner, and that says it all; once she has been there, she forgets all else.

AGNÈS – It is true that this good lady has a most charitable heart. But who is this gentleman or lady prisoner whom she has gone to visit, and of whom you speak so ambiguously?

ANGÉLIQUE – I am right to speak in this way, for it is the most comic ambiguity that has ever been heard of; but the riddle is entirely solved, and I was already going to tell you, without beating about the bush, that Madame is with her gentleman prisoner.

AGNÈS – What you have just told me is so much of a riddle for me that I can understand nothing. But I can see that something new has happened, and the Abbess is deeply involved in it; I am burning with impatience to know every detail; hurry up and tell me, and do not leave me yearning.

ANGÉLIQUE – I can see that you are asleep while others are awake, and that you are still a novice in this profession of ours.

AGNÈS – Not as much as you might think; and when I tell you of what has been happening since I saw you, you will be forced to admit that I know just as much as another girl and that, even when asleep, I put my time to very good use. But tell me, rather, the story of the prisoner.

ANGÉLIQUE – Do you know that big girl who sometimes comes to do jobs for us in the convent?

AGNÈS – You mean Madelon, I suppose – Madame's servant?

ANGÉLIQUE – No, of course not. I mean Marine, that officious girl who is always ready to serve us when we have any business with her. So just imagine that Marine is a handsome young man who, burning with love for Pasithée, and Pasithée being madly in love with him, has used this disguise to inveigle himself into our convent and satisfy his love.

AGNÈS – Tell me, I beg you, the whole story, and do not leave out a single detail out. I can sense in advance an inexpressible pleasure. Ooh, what a good-looking lad this Marine must be! It would be a shame if he were a girl. He is too strong and sinewy to share the weaknesses of our sex.

ANGÉLIQUE – You will better be able to judge when you have learned all the rest, which I will now tell you little by little. So then, this young scamp, who had set his heart on our young she-rabbits, and who was especially intent on Sister Pasithée, found the means, in this new shape, of entering our burrow.[6]

Agnès – God knows what ravages this cunning fox will have carried out, unless Pasithée has always kept him at her side; not a day goes by without him coming to offer his services, and I remember that we sometimes kept him busy for weeks at a time.

Angélique – I can assure you that he has thoroughly managed to make the most of the opportunity, and that only two doleful sisters have not experienced his vigour. I know from experience that he wields his crossbow very effectively, and I have yet to see a Carmelite or Cordelier who can equal him in his amorous combats.

Agnès – You make my mouth water when I hear you talking like that.

Angélique – I do not think that he would have forgotten you, and that you would not have had your share of him, if a certain misfortune had not befallen.

Agnès – I pity that poor unfortunate, without exactly knowing his misfortune.

Angélique – You must also pity the whole society, which lost a great deal when it lost this valiant champion.

Agnès – To tell you the truth, I pity myself, and would not be displeased to discover for myself whether this boy is as valiant as you say. But too bad! I cannot stop myself interrupting you, however desirous I am of hearing the rest of this story. So do finish, my dear Angélique. Tell me how it was discovered that Marine was a boy disguised as a girl, since all the nuns had an equal interest in concealing this fact.

Angélique – It is true, my dear Agnès, that a girl of that kind was a treasure for a convent such as ours. But how could such a precious treasure be possessed by so many nuns at the same time, without discord and envy looming? There is not girl who did not always want to keep Marine busy when they knew of what she was capable. Pasithée, who was the first in possession, wanted him all to herself. She said that the others could not dispute her claim to a possession that rightfully belonged to her; that it was for love of her that Marine exposed herself every day to a manifest danger; that she alone possessed her heart, that nobody had any right over her body, and that it was quite enough for the rest to be able to enjoy whatever was left over. The other sisters refused to accept these arguments. As you know, when somebody is hungry, and sees a nice piece of meat, they cannot bear it to be cut into pieces so that they are just handed the scraps and leftovers, since, as you can well believe, when that Sir Marin had passed through Pasithée's hands, her strength was already exhausted – and this was not at all to the liking of the professed sisters, who all want the first and best morsels for themselves.

AGNÈS – But tell me, how were they able to discover that Marine was a boy?

ANGÉLIQUE – Well now… Pasithée, who was at that time in full possession of him, one day summoned Marine into her room to make her bed, claiming that she was ill, and kept her for a whole hour, and you can imagine how they spent that hour. Meanwhile, Sister Catherine entered Pasithée's room, the door of which was ajar, and saw some happenings that gave her a strange sensation of surprise. She asked Sister Pasithée if this was how Marine helped her to make her bed, which seemed really rather rumpled. Pasithée tried to conceal her misdeed by saying that she had gone to bed to rest, but that her illness had given her such great discomfort that she had fidgeted and shifted place twenty times over, hence the rumpled bed; Marine, taking pity on her malady, had not wished to leave her room until she could see that she was somewhat recovered. Sister Catherine pretended to believe what Pasithée had just told her; but what she had seen with her own eyes did not enable her to doubt that Marine was a most handsome boy in the clothes of a young girl. Delighted by such a happy discovery, her thoughts were now bent on making the most of such a wonderful opportunity. However, as I have already told you, she thought it best to dissimulate, and let Pasithée think that she had bought her story and fallen for the pretence. 'Pull the other one!' said Catherine to herself; 'a handsome bird like *that* is not going to escape my clutches without me pulling a feather or two off him!' Her deeds matched her thoughts. After leaving Pasithée's room, telling Marine to leave too, since Pasithée needed to be left in peace and quiet, she took this so-called girl by the hand and, leading her to her own room, told her she needed a small service from her. After closing the door, she asked Marine to unlace her, saying that her skirt was much too tight. When this had been done, she told Marine that her skin was itching in several parts of her body that she could not reach, and she requested her to scratch them; this would give her great pleasure. The officious Marine performed her task with the greatest zeal – so much to the satisfaction of the girl who had made this request that she in turn started to feel a certain itch that was not at all the kind of itch usually felt by a girl. Catherine, who noticed as much, and realised that her charms were starting to have their desired effect, laid her hand as if by accident on a certain part of Marine's body; this provided her with final proof of what she had seen in Pasithée's room. Her first response was to fall over back-wards, and Marin – for so we must now call her – decided to take advantage of this new opportunity, and there occurred

between them a scene that was no less agreeable than the
one that had occurred in Pasithée's room; for, apart from
the fact that Sister Catherine is very pleasant, you know that
a change is as good as a feast.[7]

AGNÈS – That Marin must be an incomparable man –
satisfying two nuns at almost the same time

ANGÉLIQUE – He has satisfied a great number of others, whom
he has served with a great deal of pious zeal; but since he
could not suffice for all of them, there are some who are displeased, and this was the cause of his misfortune, or rather
the misfortune of all those good nuns whom he served with
such indefatigable labour.

AGNÈS – I have to admit that I am more interested in Marin
than in all the nuns put together, and I cannot bear it that
his labours were so badly rewarded. Finally, although he
has not rendered any service to me, his misfortune touches
me more than the loss suffered by all those sisters.

ANGÉLIQUE – He is, perhaps, not so much to be pitied as you
think, as you will be able to judge when I have told you the
whole story.

AGNÈS – So tell me, without any further delay, who are those
ill-intentioned girls who discovered the secret

ANGÉLIQUE – Well, this good servant was awaited by two nuns
whom he had arranged to meet, being unable to defend
himself from their importunities. But he could not come to
the assignation with either the one nor the other, since his
dear Pasithée, with whom he was, detained him for longer
than he had expected. And since there is nothing more
impatient than love, the time of the first assignation passed,
and the woman waiting for Marin saw that he had not come,
and concluded that he had forgotten all about her in the
company of another woman, or that he did not care a thing

for her. However, she continued to await him, filled with disquiet; finally, unable to remain in bed, she jumped out of it like a fury, and went round the whole convent two or three times, to try and find out what had happened. It was just one hour after midnight – the time arranged for the second assignation, at which the other nun was awaiting her dear Marin with the same impatience. And when she heard the noise made by the steps of the nun who had jumped from her bed, she did not doubt that it was her lover who had come to the assignation. With this sweet thought in mind, she opened the door of her room, which corresponded with the cloister down which her rival was walking and trying to discover, as I said, whether the man who had deceived her would appear. So, seeing this other nun's door opening, she thought it was her perfidious lover who was about to emerge after entertaining himself with another woman. She was preparing herself to deliver the most bitter rebukes to him, but when she saw that he was not coming out, although the door had been opened, she imagined that the noise she made as she walked down the cloister was stopping him from emerging, and this was perfectly plausible. So, seeing that the door was still open, she went into the room to shed more light on her anxieties. The other nun who, as I have already said, was awaiting Marin at just this time, on seeing entering into her room a person in a chemise, had not doubt but that it was he. She received him, as you can well imagine, with great transports of joy, and immediately went over and flung her arms round him. The apparent Marin, feeling himself hugged so tightly by his rival, thought that this was a manoeuvre to enable the lover to escape more easily, and, pulling herself out of the nun's arms, started looking for her unfaithful lover; but all in vain. Then there was the most comical scene imaginable between these two nuns, each of them wandering where Marin was, and neither of them having him in their power. Although both of them were right, that did not stop them quarrelling. The first continued to believe that Marin had just come out of the room where her rival had been detaining him, and the latter thought that the former, aroused by her jealousy, had prevented this assignation and, by her presence, obliged Marin to withdraw. The most comical thing of all was the way this poor nun, who was awaiting her man at just that time, saw instead a woman whom she embraced with as much ardour as if she had been the man she was awaiting.

AGNÈS – That means, in good French, that instead of a dagger, she found nothing but a scabbard; a strange *quid pro quo*.

ANGÉLIQUE – Dead right.

AGNÈS – However greatly I desire to know the end of the story, I cannot help interrupting you, to tell you of a turn of events that will make you laugh; thinking of the scabbard has just reminded me of it.

ANGÉLIQUE – Since we have only our entertainment at heart, and moreover have plenty of time, you can say whatever you wish, and you speak with such wit and in such an agreeable manner that I am delighted to hear you.

AGNÈS – Enough with the compliments already. I will need just a few words to say what I have to say. So then: my uncle had set off to travel through the main cities in France, merely for his own pleasure, and he stopped awhile in the city of Toulouse, so as to have enough time to take in what will most repay the curiosity of strangers. One morning he went to the law courts, and since he knew that he would need to take off his sword there, and so as to avoid the insults of the lackeys who have the right to remove it from all those who set foot in the courtyard without having taken it off, he did not fail to observe a law that is observed by the greatest nobles. So as soon as he was at the entrance to the courtyard, he left his sword with a merchant of his acquaintance, and kept merely his scabbard, which he always carried with his baldric, as was the fashion at the time. So he entered the courtyard, holding his left hand on his scabbard, at the place where the handguard is, as if to prevent anyone coming to seize it from him. No sooner had he been spotted than a host of lackeys flung themselves on him and, judging of the value of the sword from the beauty of the baldric that they saw this gentleman wearing, they thought they would be seizing a precious beauty if they took his sword away from him, since they were not allowed to take the baldric. So, making a grab at the sword which they thought was in the scabbard, and which my uncle could not prevent them from taking, they started fighting over who should have it, and threw themselves pell-mell on that wretched scabbard, tearing it into a thousand pieces, not knowing who had actually got hold of it. My uncle watched them and laughed, in the secret of his heart, at this squabble between over two hundred lackeys who, like famished dogs, were barking after their prey. With an innocent air, he said to them: '*Gentlemen, I know that my sword belongs to you, and unfortunately for me, I forgot to leave it when I entered this courtyard, but if you will ensure that the man who took it returns it to me, here are two louis d'or all ready for you to go and drink to my health.*' Such an honest plan merely drove those rascals into an even worse fury against each other; each of them accused his companion of having concealed the sword in some hidden place; meanwhile my uncle withdrew, and left them to sort out as best they could this comical quarrel that had made them mistake a scabbard for a sword.

ANGÉLIQUE – The same applied to our nuns, when they thought they had Marin in their grasp. Their squabble became so heated that the Abbess heard the whole din. Since she had a long experience of the tricks that love can play, she did not doubt that this was another amorous imbroglio. She first roused her servant Madelon, ordered her to light her candle and, rising dressed just in her chemise, since it was during the great hot months of summer, she went off to see what it was. The first thing that she saw from afar was Marin slipping out of Pasithée's room; having heard the uproar, and concluding that he was the main cause of it, he went to snuggle down in his own bed. The Abbess saw him pass and disappear at almost one and the same time, and did not know who he was; she merely decided, by virtue of his gait, that he had to be a man; but, not knowing where to find him, she went off to inspect all the nuns' rooms in an attempt to find out what she could. However, the two nuns who had been frustrated in their wait were caught in the act by Madame while their quarrel was at its most heated, and since they had one and the same interest in concealing the cause of their dispute, this storm subsided as soon as the Abbess appeared. But since it was not easy to pull the wool over her eyes, and since these two nuns seemed to her to be very agitated, she concluded that there was something extraordinary afoot on which light would soon be shed. She did not waste her time in questioning them, or in asking them why they were not both in their rooms, nor who that phantom was which had appeared and disappeared at the same time: she knew that they would not be lacking in inventions to conceal all their follies; she thought that the quickest thing would be to go and ferret around everywhere and to inspect all the beds and all the rooms. Since she was an old hand at this game, she imagined that she would discover some clue that would reveal this mystery to her, in which she already knew that several nuns were involved, especially Pasithée, from whose room she had seen the phantom emerging, and the two angry sisters.

AGNÈS –Tell me, I beg you, before continuing, who those sisters were who were so frustrated.

ANGÉLIQUE – I am amazed you have taken so long to ask me that; but since you wish to know, I will tell you without beating about the bush that *I* was the women to whom the first assignation was given, and that it is why I know all the details better than anyone else; and Sister Colette was the woman who was to have the second assignation.

AGNÈS – So you are the main cause of the misfortune that occurred.

ANGÉLIQUE – Just say that I am the occasion of it; and indeed, no damage would have been done, if we had not had such a penetrating Abbess, who used the most bizarre means that could come to the mind of a melancholy old woman.

AGNÈS – Do finish your story, then, I beg you: I am impatiently awaiting the end of it.

ANGÉLIQUE – The first thing that our Abbess did was to make sure of Colette and myself, and to order us to stay with her until she had done all that she purposed.

AGNÈS – She doubtless feared lest you go to warn the others to be on their guard or lets you help the thief to make his escape.

ANGÉLIQUE – Precisely.

AGNÈS – The cunning old vixen!

ANGÉLIQUE – She first went to knock on Pasithée's door. Pasithée was pretending to be asleep and it was some time before she responded. Finally, hearing that the knocking continued, and hearing Madame's voice, she jumped out of bed and went to open the door. The Abbess resolutely told her that she wished to inspect the whole convent that very minute, and that she was certain that there was a man hiding somewhere in it. Pasithée, apparently most surprised at what the Abbess had just said, made five or six signs of the cross, and said *Jesus Maria!* over a score of times. The Abbess, who walked straight in, wanted to look under the bed and examine Sister Pasithée from her head to her feet. She examined first the sheets, and then the chemise, and eventually recognised the fresh traces of a man; and having displayed this evidence to us, said, 'You can see that the wolf has been in the sheep-fold! We merely have to find him: he will not be able to escape, for I have the keys to all the doors, and the walls are so high that he cannot climb over them'. These words made us shudder, especially Pasithée, who was the most deeply implicated. However, managing to control her anxieties, she maintained that no man had entered her room. 'You must mean that it was a woman, then,' said the Abbess, 'for you cannot deny that a person in nothing but a chemise came out of your room, not a quarter of an hour ago, since I saw her myself.'

'That is true,' she said, 'but that was Marine, who had come to serve me in my last illness, as Sister Catherine knows very well, and was now here to see how I was feeling, for she had heard me complaining all day long.'

'Well!' said the Abbess, 'I believe what you are telling me; however, we will see whether Marine is not some marine monster in search of human flesh, similar to the one who gave me such a fright a few nights ago.'

These last words were the final blow for Sister Pasithée, although Madame had uttered them at random, and although the idea that Marine was a man could not have occurred to her. After this, giving no time to Pasithée or to us to dress, she ordered her to follow; walking ahead, with Madelon holding a candle, she went to knock on Catherine's door. Catherine had already awoken at the noise we were making, and quickly came to open up to us. The Abbess did her the same favour that she had already bestowed upon Pasithée and examined her in turn; she found that she was no cleaner than the other nun, although the traces were not so recent. 'Oh!' she said. 'Oh! This is a wolf that has been going around this house for some days, and he already knows what creatures dwell herein; let us continue to follow his tracks: we will eventually find him.' After that, she left Catherine's room, ordering her to follow along with us. And thus, trooping along from room to room, our number grew ever bigger, and Madame continued to find new traces of her wolf. 'Well now!' she said, 'this beast is ravenous – and he likes to change his lair!' After that, she told us something that we would never have expected. '*You know, my daughters,*' said she, '*that Satan sometimes changes himself into an angel of light, and ravening wolves sometimes assume the fleeces of sheep. We must find out whether one of us is not this wolf in disguise, causing all the ravages of which you have seen the marks; for if it were not a wolf in disguise, he would not have the leisure to do all that he does do.*' So saying, she pulled up her chemise and showed us all that God had given her. 'You can see,' she told us, showing us a body as white as snow, 'that I am an angel of light.' When this had been done, she wanted us all to do likewise; there were some who were more than reluctant, but they had to undergo this examination. 'I am delighted,' she said to us then, 'that you are merely what you seem to be, but it is still certain that several of you have welcomed the wolf into their fold. Let us go now,' she said, 'to the quarters of the novice sisters.'

AGNÈS – That is what I wanted to hear, for, being one of the number, I wanted to know how Madame could have forgotten us.

ANGÉLIQUE – That was not necessary, as you will see from what I tell you. As you know, on the way from the quarter of the professed sisters to that of the novices, you have to pass through a kind of attic that serves as a room for the women who come to help us sweep out the convent. This was just where Marin was lying on a scruffy mattress. The Abbess, who suddenly remembered what Pasithée had told her, namely that Marine was the only person who had entered her room, said, 'So that we will have nothing to reproach ourselves with, since we find ourselves outside Marine's room, we must ascertain whether *she* was perhaps that angel of Satan who comes the disturb the nuns' rest in the middle of the night.' Thereupon, one of the nuns who had an interest in Marin not being recognised for who he was, pointed out to the Abbess that it was not right to divulge the secrets of the cloister in this way, and that a girl who was not a member of their society, nor even their domestic servant, should not be apprised of the suspicions going round that a man had entered the convent. 'Whatever,' said the Abbess. 'Marine is still going to undergo the examination just like the others, and with even greater rigour, since, as Pasithée herself has said, she entered her room this very night.' At these terrible words, Pasithée very nearly dropped dead at the Abbess's feet. Finally they entered Marine's room: the door did not have any bolt, and was merely closed with a latch. Who could express Marin's surprise on seeing Madelon come in holding a candle, and the Abbess with twenty nuns all in chemises! This procession had something strangely funereal about it, and she was taken aback; and when the Abbess noticed this, she said, 'Marine, do not be afraid: it is just a little formality that has brought us here. We are looking for a man who has hidden himself in here, and just as at night all cats are grey, and that there is nothing that more resembles a tomcat than a female pussy, we need to see whether you are male or female, for as you know, the habit does not make the nun. We can see that you are wearing a woman's dress, but we want to see if you are woman from your head to your toes.' Marine replied grumbling that they should let her sleep, she had been working all day, she needed rest, and was in no mood to hear of these larks. The Abbess, who refused to leave things as they stood, gently pointed out that she would have to yield and undergo the test, and that she must not have any advantage over the professed sisters who had been forced to do the same. Some of the nuns then said that they would not be displeased if Marine were left alone, and that she could enjoy her rest without anyone feeling envious at her privilege of not being examined. 'It is a fine pleasure,' said another, 'for nuns to see the filthy, mangy body of a horrid servant girl!' All this merely increased the curiosity of the Abbess, and confirmed her suspicions. At the same time, she noticed that Pasithée was more dead than alive, and Catherine, Colette and I appeared really rather worried. 'Very well!' she said, 'if you wish to spare yourselves the sight of this servant girl's body, you need merely close your eyes, and I will proceed to examine her.'

So saying, she took the candle from Madelon and ordered her to stand aside. Poor Marin did all that he could to conceal what nature had given him, and his fear then came to his aid; but although fear can freeze our limbs, it cannot destroy them entirely. Finally he stood there like a dog threatened with a beating, and hiding his tail between his legs. I had forgotten to tell you that, while the Abbess and the nuns were involved in this comical disputation, had taken one of his garters and made a kind of bridle from it, which he attached to the end of his thingy, and, passing it under his thighs, pinned the other end of the garter behind his back, under his chemise. Meanwhile Madame, having uncovered him in front, could still see nothing womanly about him. She did note, however, that Marin was crossing his legs in such a way that she guessed this was not the effect of modesty alone; so she wanted to take a closer look, and, since she is extremely short-sighted, she used her spectacles, adjusting them on her nose as if she were about to inspect precious rarity or some valuable piece of jewellery. As she was proceeding to a more ample verification of the evidence, and practically leaning her spectacles against Marine's stomach as if it had been a bookstand on which she had placed her breviary, during all this time, well, the member that Marin was trying so carefully to conceal, and that seems to stiffen whenever it encounters resistance, did indeed stiffen so much, as a result of Marin trying to constrain it, that it all of a sudden sprung out erect, hitting the Abbess's spectacles right in the middle, making them fly up into the canopy over the bed, smashing them to pieces and with the same great wallop extinguishing the candle that she was holding. The good lady, who had long known what men look like, no longer doubted that Marin was one of them, and, placing her hand on what had dealt her this terrible blow, was so surprised that, instead of one man, she concluded that he must, at the very least, be a man and a half. The nuns, who had not observed so closely what was happening, and who saw that the candle had gone out, had various ideas on the matter: those who knew Marin *intus et in cute*[8] realised the truth of the matter; other deduced that, in order to ward off this shameful inspection, he had knocked the Abbess's candle and glasses away with his hand. Finally there were some good sisters, of those illuminated souls who are forever desirous of seeing miracles in everything, who said that it was Saint Clare, the patron saint of the convent, who, unable to tolerate the chaste girls of the society being suspected of unchastity, was visibly expressing her displeasure at an inspection that implied such dishonour for their order. The Abbess knew full well what to believe; nonetheless, pretending to agree with this conclusion, she said that, since this misfortune had occurred, since the torch had gone out and her spectacles had been broken (she did not know how), she would not continue with her inspection; but since Marine had given rise to all this hue and cry, by entering at night, without any need, Pasithée's room, she would be placed in solitary confinement for a few days in a separate room, to which Madame would have the key, and she would not be able to leave without Madame's permission; however, she expressly forbade us to speak to the novices, nor to the boarders, nor indeed to anyone in the outside world about what had passed between her and us. You can easily guess, dear Agnès, why she so insistently urged us to keep this secret, and the reason why she is obliged to lock Marin away in a separate room.

AGNÈS – She found this bird so handsome, in her view, that she wishes to lock him away in a cage to serve her every least pleasure.

ANGÉLIQUE – She decided that nuns like us did not deserve such a fine morsel, which was fit only for an Abbess. I do not know whether Marin is pleased at his fate; but I do know that he is missed by more than one nun.

AGNÈS – He will not be in prison forever.

ANGÉLIQUE – No, but the Abbess's eyes will keep him in their sight.

AGNÈS – It has to be admitted, Angélique, that you have given me considerable pleasure by telling me such an unusual story.

ANGÉLIQUE – Tell me, Agnès, in turn, what you have to tell me about your latest adventures. You mentioned that, even while asleep, you had made good use of your time. It must be something really amusing.

AGNÈS – Much more than I can say; but it is time, we are being summoned to the service, and we must postpone this until the next conversation.

ANGÉLIQUE – Kiss me, then, my sweetest heart, while I await this pleasure from you.

NOTES

1. The sister in charge of the convent's external relations.
2. Basin used for washing hands at the offertory in the Catholic Mass – also the name for the ritual action itself.
3. My sweet Lord Jesus, do me the grace…
4. A true light for love.
5. The text seems corrupt here: it says merely 'lui', which can mean 'to him' or 'to her', and the adjective 'indulgent' in the next line is, in the French, feminine, as if the bundle were being given to Alios herself. But the situation, and the subsequent narrative, suggest that this cannot be so.
6. The French word for 'warren' or 'burrow' here (*'clapier'*) could also mean a brothel.
7. The French says: '*à nouvelle viande nouvel appétit*', 'with fresh meat comes new appetite'.
8. Intimately (Latin).

BIOGRAPHICAL NOTE

Andrew Brown studied at the University of Cambridge, where he taught French for many years. He now works as a freelance teacher and translator, and is the author of *Roland Barthes: the Figures of Writing* (OUP, 1993). His translations for Hesperus include classic texts such as Zola's *For a Night of Love*, Voltaire's *Memoirs of the Life of Monsieur de Voltaire*, and Dumas's *The Corsican Brothers*, and works of contemporary fiction such as Laurent Gaudé's *The Scortas' Sun*, Yasmine Ghata's *The Calligraphers' Night* and Jacques-Pierre Amette's *Brecht's Lover*.